Tales for a Winter's Night

Arthur Conan Doyle

Tales for a Winter's Night

ACADEMY

CHICAGO

This edition copyright © 1989 by
Academy Chicago Publishers
An imprint of Chicago Review Press, Incorporated
814 North Franklin Street
Chicago, Illinois 60610

ISBN 978-0-89733-309-2

Cover design: Sarah Olson
Cover art: *Les trois commères*, H. Daumier

Library of Congress Cataloging-in-Publication Data

Doyle, Arthur Conan, Sir, 1859–1930.
      Tales for a winter's night.

      Contents: The man with the watches
      —The black doctor
      —The Jew's breastplate—[etc.]
      I. Detective and mystery stories, English. I. Title.
PR4621 1988 823'.8 87-33499
ISBN 0-89733-309-8 (pbk.)

/ Preface /

In the present volume have been assembled a number of mystery stories such as might well be read "round the fire" upon a winter's night. This would be my ideal atmosphere for such stories, if an author might choose his time and place as an artist does the light and hanging of his picture. However, if they have the good fortune to give pleasure to anyone, at any time or place, their author will be very satisfied.

ACD

/ Contents /

/ The Man With the Watches /

There are many who will still bear in mind the singular circumstances which, under the heading of the Rugby Mystery, filled many columns of the daily Press in the spring of the year 1892. Coming as it did at a period of exceptional dulness, it attracted perhaps rather more attention than it deserved, but it offered to the public that mixture of the whimsical and the tragic which is most stimulating to the popular imagination. Interest drooped, however, when, after weeks of fruitless investigation, it was found that no final explanation of the facts was forthcoming, and the tragedy seemed from that time to the present to have finally taken its place in the dark catalogue of inexplicable and unexpiated crimes. A recent communication (the authenticity of which appears to be above question) has, however, thrown some new and clear light upon the matter. Before laying it before the public it would be as well, perhaps, that I should refresh their memories as to the singular facts upon which this commentary is founded. These facts were briefly as follows:—

At five o'clock on the evening of the 18th of March in the year already mentioned a train left Euston Station for

Manchester. It was a rainy, squally day, which grew wilder as it progressed, so it was by no means the weather in which any one would travel who was not driven to do so by necessity. The train, however, is a favourite one among Manchester business men who are returning from town, for it does the journey in four hours and twenty minutes, with only three stoppages upon the way. In spite of the inclement evening it was, therefore, fairly well filled upon the occasion of which I speak. The guard of the train was a tried servant of the company—a man who had worked for twenty-two years without blemish or complaint. His name was John Palmer.

The station clock was upon the stroke of five, and the guard was about to give the customary signal to the engine-driver when he observed two belated passengers hurrying down the platform. The one was an exceptionally tall man, dressed in a long black overcoat with Astrakhan collar and cuffs. I have already said that the evening was an inclement one, and the tall traveller had the high, warm collar turned up to protect his throat against the bitter March wind. He appeared, as far as the guard could judge by so hurried an inspection, to be a man between fifty and sixty years of age, who had retained a good deal of the vigour and activity of his youth. In one hand he carried a brown leather Gladstone bag. His companion was a lady, tall and erect, walking with a vigorous step which outpaced the gentleman beside her. She wore a long, fawn-coloured dust-cloak, a black, close-fitting toque, and a dark veil which concealed the greater part of her face. The two might very well have passed as father and daughter. They walked swiftly down the line of carriages, glancing in at the windows, until the guard, John Palmer, overtook them.

"Now, then, sir, look sharp, the train is going," said he.

"First-class," the man answered.

The guard turned the handle of the nearest door. In the carriage, which he had opened, there sat a small man with a cigar in his mouth. His appearance seems to have impressed itself upon the guard's memory, for he was prepared, afterwards, to describe or to identify him. He was a man of thirty-four or thirty-five years of age, dressed in some grey material, sharp-nosed, alert, with a ruddy, weather-beaten face, and a small, closely cropped black beard. He glanced up as the door was opened. The tall man paused with his foot upon the step.

"This is a smoking compartment. The lady dislikes smoke," said he, looking round at the guard.

"All right! Here you are, sir!" said John Palmer. He slammed the door of the smoking carriage, opened that of the next one, which was empty, and thrust the two travellers in. At the same moment he sounded his whistle and the wheels of the train began to move, The man with the cigar was at the window of his carriage, and said something to the guard as he rolled past him, but the words were lost in the bustle of the departure. Palmer stepped into the guard's van, as it came up to him, and thought no more of the incident.

Twelve minutes after its departure the train reached Willesden Junction, where it stopped for a very short interval. An examination of the tickets has made it certain that no one either joined or left it at this time, and no passenger was seen to alight upon the platform. At 5.14 the journey to Manchester was resumed, and Rugby was reached at 6.50, the express being five minutes late.

At Rugby the attention of the station officials was drawn to the fact that the door of one of the first-class carriages was open. An examination of that compartment, and of its neighbour, disclosed a remarkable state of affairs.

The smoking carriage in which the short, red-faced man with the black beard had been seen was now empty. Save for a half-smoked cigar, there was no trace whatever of its recent occupant. The door of this carriage was fastened. In the next compartment, to which attention had been originally drawn, there was no sign either of the gentleman with the Astrakhan collar or of the young lady who accompanied him. All three passengers had disappeared. On the other hand, there was found upon the floor of this carriage—the one in which the tall traveller and the lady had been—a young man, fashionably dressed and of elegant appearance. He lay with his knees drawn up, and his head resting against the further door, an elbow upon either seat. A bullet had penetrated his heart and his death must have been instantaneous. No one had seen such a man enter the train, and no railway ticket was found in his pocket, neither were there any markings upon his linen, nor papers nor personal property which might help to identify him. Who he was, whence he had come, and how he had met his end were each as great a mystery as what had occurred to the three people who had started an hour and a half before from Willesden in those two compartments.

I have said that there was no personal property which might help to identify him, but it is true that there was one peculiarity about this unknown young man which was much commented upon at the time. In his pockets were found no fewer than six valuable gold watches, three in the various pockets of his waistcoat, one in his ticket-pocket, one in his breast pocket, and one small one set in a leather strap and fastened round his left wrist. The obvious explanation that the man was a pickpocket, and that this was his plunder, was discounted by the fact that all six were of American make, and of a type which is rare in England. Three of them bore the mark of the Rochester Watchmaking Company; one was by Mason, of Elmira; one was unmarked; and the small one, which was highly jewelled and ornamented, was from Tiffany, of New York. The other contents of his pocket consisted of an ivory knife with a corkscrew by Rodgers, of Sheffield; a small circular mirror, one inch in diameter; a re-admission slip to the Lyceum theatre; a silver box full of vesta matches, and a brown leather cigar-case containing two cheroots—also two pounds fourteen shillings in money. It was clear, then, that whatever motives may have led to his death, robbery was not among them. As already mentioned, there were no markings upon the man's linen, which appeared to be new, and no tailor's name upon his coat. In appearance he was young, short, smooth-cheeked, and delicately featured. One of his front teeth was conspicuously stopped with gold,

On the discovery of the tragedy an examination was instantly made of the tickets of all passengers, and the number of the passengers themselves was counted. It was found that only three tickets were unaccounted for, corresponding to the three travellers who were missing. The express was then allowed to proceed, but a new guard was sent with it, and John Palmer was detained as a witness at Rugby. The carriage which included the two compartments in question was uncoupled and side-tracked. Then, on the arrival of Inspector Vane, of Scotland Yard, and of Mr. Henderson, a detective in the service of the railway company, an exhaustive inquiry was made into all the circumstances.

That a crime had been committed was certain. The bullet, which appeared to have come from a small pistol or revolver, had been fired from some little distance, as there was no scorching of the clothes. No weapon was found in the compartment (which finally disposed of the theory of suicide), nor was there any sign of the brown leather bag which the guard had seen in the hand of the tall gentleman. A lady's parasol was found upon the rack, but no other trace was to be seen of the travellers in either of the sections. Apart from the crime, the question of how or why three passengers (one of them a lady) could get out of the train, and one other get in during the unbroken run between Willesden and Rugby, was one which excited the utmost curiosity among the general public, and gave rise to much speculation in the London Press.

John Palmer, the guard, was able at the inquest to give some evidence which threw a little light upon the matter. There was a spot between Tring and Cheddington, according to his statement, where, on account of some repairs to the line, the train had for a few minutes slowed down to a pace not exceeding eight or ten miles an hour. At that place it might be possible for a man, or even for an exceptionally active woman, to have left the train without serious injury. It was true that a gang of platelayers was there, and that they had seen nothing, but it was their custom to stand in the middle between the metals, and the open carriage door was upon the far side, so that it was conceivable that someone might have alighted unseen, as the darkness would by that time be drawing in. A steep embankment would instantly screen anyone who sprang out from the observation of the navvies.

The guard also deposed that there was a good deal of movement upon the platform at Willesden Junction, and that though it was certain that no one had either joined or left the train there, it was still quite possible that some of the passengers might have changed unseen from one compartment to another. It was by no means uncommon for a gentleman to finish his cigar in a smoking carriage and then to change to a clearer atmosphere. Supposing that the man with the black beard had done so at Willesden (and the half-smoked cigar upon the floor seemed to favour the supposition), he would naturally go into the nearest section, which would bring him into the company of the two other actors in this drama. Thus the first stage of the affair might be surmised without any great breach of probability. But what the second stage had been, or how the final one had been arrived at, neither the guard nor the experienced detective officers could suggest.

A careful examination of the line between Willesden and Rugby resulted in one discovery which might or might not have a bearing upon the tragedy. Near Tring, at the very place where the train slowed down, there was found at the bottom of the embankment a small pocket Testament, very shabby and worn. It was printed by the Bible Society of London, and bore an inscription: "From John to Alice. Jan. 13th, 1856," upon the fly-leaf. Underneath was written: "James, July 4th, 1859," and beneath that again: "Edward. Nov. 1st, 1869," all the entries being in the same handwriting. This was the only clue, if it could be called a clue, which the police obtained, and the coroner's verdict of "Murder by a person or persons unknown" was the unsatisfactory ending of a singular case. Advertisement, rewards, and inquiries proved equally fruitless, and nothing could be found which was solid enough to form the basis for a profitable investigation.

It would be a mistake, however, to suppose that no theories were formed to account for the facts. On the contrary, the Press, both in England and in America, teemed with suggestions and suppositions, most of which were obviously absurd. The fact that the watches were of American make, and some peculiarities in connection with the gold stopping of his front tooth, appeared to indicate that the deceased was a citizen of the United States, though his linen, clothes, and boots were undoubtedly of British manufacture. It was surmised, by some, that he was concealed under the seat, and that, being discovered, he was for some reason, possibly because he had overheard their guilty secrets, put to death by his fellow-passengers. When coupled with generalities as to the ferocity and cunning of anarchical and other secret societies, this theory sounded as plausible as any.

The fact that he should be without a ticket would be consistent with the idea of concealment, and it was well known that women played a prominent part in the Nihilistic propaganda. On the other hand, it was clear, from the guard's statement, that the man must have been hidden there *before* the others arrived, and how unlikely the coincidence that conspirators should stray exactly into the very compartment in which a spy was already concealed! Besides, this explanation ignored the man in the smoking carriage, and gave no reason at all for his simultaneous disappearance. The police had little difficulty in showing that such a theory would not cover the facts, but they were unprepared in the absence of evidence to advance any alternative explanation.

There was a letter in the *Daily Gazette,* over the signature of a well-known criminal investigator, which gave rise to considerable discussion at the time. He had formed a hypothesis which had at least ingenuity to recommend it, and I cannot do better than append it in his own words.

"Whatever may be the truth," said he, "it must depend upon some bizarre and rare combination of events, so we need have no hesitation in postulating such events in our explanation. In the absence of data we must abandon the analytic or scientific method of investigation, and must approach it in the synthetic fashion. In a word, instead of taking known events and deducing from them what has occurred, we must build up a fanciful explanation if it will only be consistent with known events. We can then test this explanation by any fresh facts which may arise. If they all fit into their places, the probability is that we are upon the right track, and with each fresh fact this probability increases in a geometrical progression until the evidence becomes final and convincing.

"Now, there is one most remarkable and suggestive fact which has not met with the attention which it deserves. There is a local train running through Harrow and King's Langley, which is timed in such a way that the express must have overtaken it at or about the period when it eased down its speed to eight miles an hour on account of the repairs of the line. The two trains would at that time be travelling in the same direction at a similar rate of speed and upon parallel lines. It is within everyone's experience how, under such circumstances, the occupant of each carriage can see very plainly the passengers in the other carriages opposite to him. The lamps of the express had been lit at Willesden, so that each compartment was brightly illuminated, and most visible to an observer from outside.

"Now, the sequence of events as I reconstruct them would be after this fashion. This young man with the abnormal number of watches was alone in the carriage of the slow train. His ticket, with his papers and gloves and other things, was, we will suppose, on the seat beside him. He was probably an American, and also probably a man of weak intellect. The excessive wearing of jewellery is an early symptom in some forms of mania.

"As he sat watching the carriages of the express which were (on account of the state of the line) going at the same pace as himself, he suddenly saw some people in it whom he knew. We will suppose for the sake of our theory that these people were a woman whom he loved and a man whom he hated—and who in return hated him. The young man was excitable and impulsive. He opened the door of his carriage, stepped from the footboard of the local train to the footboard of the express, opened the other door, and made his way into the presence of these two people. The feat (on the supposition that the trains were going at the same pace) is by no means so perilous as it might appear.

"Having now got our young man without his ticket into the carriage in which the elder man and the young woman are travelling, it is not difficult to imagine that a violent scene ensued. It is possible that the pair were also Americans, which is the more probable as the man carried a weapon—an unusual thing in England. If our supposition of incipient mania is correct, the young man is likely to have assaulted the other. As the upshot of the quarrel the elder man shot the intruder, and then made his escape from the carriage, taking the young lady with him. We will suppose that all this happened very rapidly, and that the train was still going at so slow a pace that it was not difficult for them to leave it. A woman might leave a train going at eight miles an hour. As a matter of fact, we know that this woman *did* do so.

"And now we have to fit in the man in the smoking carriage. Presuming that we have, up to this point, reconstructed the tragedy correctly, we shall find nothing in this other man to cause us to reconsider our conclusions. According to my theory, this man saw the young fellow cross from one train to the other, saw him open the door, heard the pistol-shot, saw the two fugitives spring out on to the line, realized that murder had been done, and sprang out himself in pursuit. Why he has never been heard of since—whether he met his own death in the pursuit, or whether, as is more likely, he was made to realize that it was not a case for his interference—is a detail which we have at present no means of explaining. I acknowledge that there are some difficulties in the way. At first sight, it might seem improbable that at such a moment a murderer would burden himself in his flight with a brown leather bag. My answer is that he was well aware that if the bag were found his identity would be established. It was absolutely necessary for him to take it with him. My theory stands or falls upon one point, and I call upon the railway company to make strict inquiry as to whether a ticket was found unclaimed in the local train through Harrow and King's Langley upon the 18th of March. If such a ticket were found my case is proved. If not, my theory may still be the correct one, for it is conceivable either that he travelled without a ticket or that his ticket was lost."

To this elaborate and plausible hypothesis the answer of the police and of the company was, first, that no such ticket was found; secondly, that the slow train would never run parallel to the express; and, thirdly, that the local train had been stationary in King's Langley Station when the express, going at fifty miles an hour, had flashed past it. So perished the only satisfying explanation, and five years have now elapsed without supplying a new one. Now, at last, there comes a statement which covers all the facts, and which must be regarded as authentic. It took the shape of a letter dated from New York, and addressed to the same criminal investigator whose theory I have quoted. It is given here in extenso, with the exception of the two opening paragraphs, which are personal in their nature:—

"You'll excuse me if I'm not very free with names. There's less reason now than there was five years ago when mother was still living. But for all that, I had rather cover up our tracks all I can. But I owe you an explanation, for if your idea of it was wrong, it was a mighty ingenious one all the same. I'll have to go back a little so as you may understand all about it.

"My people came from Bucks, England, and emigrated to the States in the early fifties. They settled in Rochester, in the State of New York, where my father ran a large dry goods store. There were only two sons: myself, James, and my brother Edward. I was ten years older than my brother, and after my father died I sort of took the place of a father to him, as an elder brother would. He was a bright, spirited boy, and just one of the most beautiful creatures that ever lived. But there was always a soft spot in him, and it was like mould in cheese, for it spread and spread, and nothing that you could do would stop it. Mother saw it just as clearly as I did, but she went on spoiling him all the same, for he had such a way with him that you could refuse him nothing. I did all I could to hold him in, and he hated me for my pains.

"At last he fairly got his head, and nothing that we could do would stop him. He got off into New York, and went rapidly from bad to worse. At first he was only fast, and then he was criminal; and then, at the end of a year or two, he was one of the most notorious young crooks in the city. He had formed a friendship with Sparrow MacCoy, who was at the head of his profession as a bunco-steerer, green goodsman, and general rascal. They took to card-sharping, and frequented some of the best hotels in New York. My brother was an excellent actor (he might have made an honest name for himself if he had chosen), and he would take the parts of a young Englishman of title, of a simple lad from the West, or of a college undergraduate, whichever suited Sparrow MacCoy's purpose. And then one day he dressed himself as a girl, and he carried it off so well, and made himself such a valuable decoy, that it was their favourite game afterwards. They had made it right with Tammany and with the police, so it seemed as if nothing could ever stop them, for those were in the days before the Lexow Commission, and if you only had a pull, you could do pretty nearly everything you wanted.

"And nothing would have stopped them if they had only stuck to cards and New York, but they must needs come up Rochester way, and forge a name upon a check. It was my brother that did it, though every one knew that it was under the influence of Sparrow MacCoy. I bought up that check, and a pretty sum it cost me. Then I went to my brother, laid it before him on the table, and swore to him that I would prosecute if he did not clear out of the country. At first he simply laughed. I could not prosecute, he said, without breaking our mother's heart, and he knew that I would not do that. I made him understand, however, that our mother's heart was being broken in any case, and that I had set firm on the point that I would rather see him in a Rochester gaol than in a New York hotel. So at last he gave in, and he made me a solemn promise that he would see Sparrow MacCoy no more, that he would go to Europe, and that he would turn his hand to any honest trade that I helped him to get. I took him down right away to an old family friend, Joe Willson, who is an exporter of American watches and clocks, and I got him to give Edward an agency in London, with a small salary and a 15 per cent. commission on all business. His manner and appearance were so good that he won the old man over at once, and within a week he was sent off to London with a case full of samples.

"It seemed to me that this business of the check had really given my brother a fright, and that there was some chance of his settling down into an honest line of life. My mother had spoken with him, and what she said had touched him, for she had always been the best of mothers to him, and he had been the great sorrow of her life. But I knew that this man Sparrow MacCoy had a great influence over Edward, and my chance of keeping the lad straight lay in breaking the connection between them. I had a friend in the New York detective force, and through him I kept a watch upon MacCoy. When within a fortnight of my brother's sailing I heard that MacCoy had taken a berth in the *Etruria*, I was as certain as if he had told me that he was going over to England for the purpose of coaxing Edward back again into the ways that he had left. In an instant I had resolved to go also, and to put my influence against MacCoy's. I knew it was a losing fight, but I thought, and my mother thought, that it was my duty. We passed the last night together in prayer for my success, and she gave me her own Testament that my father had given her on the day of their marriage in the Old Country, so that I might always wear it next my heart.

"I was a fellow-traveller, on the steamship, with Sparrow MacCoy, and at least I had the satisfaction of spoiling his little game for the voyage. The very first night I went into the smoking-room, and found him at the head of a card table, with half-a-dozen young fellows who were carrying their full purses and their empty skulls over to Europe. He was settling down for his harvest, and a rich one it would have been. But I soon changed all that.

"'Gentlemen,' said I, 'are you aware whom you are playing with?'

"'What's that to you? You mind your own business!' said he, with an oath.

"'Who is it, anyway?' asked one of the dudes.

"'He's Sparrow MacCoy, the most notorious card-sharper in the States.'

"Up he jumped with a bottle in his hand, but he remembered that he was under the flag of the effete Old Country, where law and order run, and Tammany has no pull. Gaol and the gallows wait for violence and murder, and there's no slipping out by the back door on board an ocean liner.

"'Prove your words, you—!' said he.

"'I will!' said I. 'If you will turn up your right shirt-sleeve to the shoulder, I will either prove my words or I will eat them.'

"He turned white and said not a word. You see, I knew something of his ways, and I was aware that part of the mechanism which he and all such sharpers use consists of an elastic down the arm with a clip just above the wrist. It is by means of this clip that they withdraw from their hands the cards which they do not want, while they substitute other cards from another hiding-place. I reckoned on it being there, and it was. He cursed me, slunk out of the saloon, and was hardly seen again during the voyage. For once, at any rate, I got level with Mister Sparrow MacCoy.

"But he soon had his revenge upon me, for when it came to influencing my brother he outweighed me every time. Edward had kept himself straight in London for the first few weeks, and had done some business with his American watches, until this villain came across his path once more. I did my best, but the best was little enough. The next thing I heard there had been a scandal at one of the Northumberland Avenue hotels: a traveller had been fleeced of a large sum by two confederate card-sharpers, and the matter was in the hands of Scotland Yard. The first I learned of it was in the evening paper, and I was at once certain that my brother and MacCoy were back at their old games. I hurried at once to Edward's lodgings. They told me that he and a tall gentleman (whom I recognized as MacCoy) had gone off together, and that he had left the lodgings and taken his things with him. The landlady had heard them give several directions to the cabman, ending with Euston Station, and she had accidentally overheard the tall gentleman saying something about Manchester. She believed that that was their destination.

"A glance at the time-table showed me that the most likely train was at five, though there was another at 4.30 which they might have caught. I had only time to get the later one, but found no sign of them either at the depot or in the train. They must have gone on by the earlier one, so I determined to follow them to Manchester and search for them in the hotels there. One last appeal to my brother by all that he owed to my mother might even now be the salvation of him. My nerves were overstrung, and I lit a cigar to steady them. At that moment, just as the train was moving off, the door of my compartment was flung open, and there were MacCoy and my brother on the platform.

"They were both disguised, and with good reason, for they knew that the London police were after them. MacCoy had a great Astrakhan collar drawn up, so that only his eyes and nose were showing. My brother was dressed like a woman, with a black veil half down his face, but of course it did not deceive me for an instant, nor would it have done so even if I had not known that he had often used such a dress before. I started up, and as I did so MacCoy recognized me. He said something, the conductor slammed the door, and they were shown into the next compartment. I tried to stop the train so as to follow them, but the wheels were already moving, and it was too late.

"When we stopped at Willesden, I instantly changed my carriage. It appears that I was not seen to do so, which is not surprising, as the station was crowded with people. MacCoy, of course, was expecting me, and he had spent the time between Euston and Willesden in saying all he could to harden my brother's heart and set him against me. That is what I fancy, for I had never found him so impossible to soften or to move. I tried this way and I tried that; I pictured his future in an English gaol; I described the sorrow of his mother when I came back with the news; I said everything to touch his heart, but all to no purpose. He sat there with a fixed sneer upon his handsome face, while every now and then Sparrow MacCoy would throw in a taunt at me, or some word of encouragement to hold my brother to his resolutions.

"'Why don't you run a Sunday-school?' he would say to me, and then, in the same breath: 'He thinks you have no will of your own. He thinks you are just the baby brother and that he can lead you where he likes. He's only just finding out that you are a man as well as he.'

"It was those words of his which set me talking bitterly. We had left Willesden, you understand, for all this took some time. My temper got the better of me, and for the first time in my life I let my brother see the rough side of me. Perhaps it would have been better had I done so earlier and more often.

"'A man!' said I. 'Well, I'm glad to have your friend's assurance of it, for no one would suspect it to see you like a boarding-school missy. I don't suppose in all this country there is a more contemptible-looking creature than you are as you sit there with that Dolly pinafore upon you.' He coloured up at that, for he was a vain man, and he winced from ridicule.

"'It's only a dust-cloak,' said he, and he slipped it off. 'One has to throw the coppers off one's scent, and I had no other way to do it.' He took his toque off with the veil attached, and he put both it and the cloak into his brown bag. 'Anyway, I don't need to wear it until the conductor comes round,' said he.

"'Nor then, either,' said I, and taking the bag I slung it with all my force out of the window. 'Now,' said I, 'you'll never make a Mary Jane of yourself while I can help it. If nothing but that disguise stands between you and a gaol, then to gaol you shall go.'

"That was the way to manage him. I felt my advantage at once. His supple nature was one which yielded to roughness far more readily than to entreaty. He flushed with shame, and his eyes filled with tears. But MacCoy saw my advantage also, and was determined that I should not pursue it.

"'He's my pard, and you shall not bully him,' he cried.

"'He's my brother, and you shall not ruin him,' said I. 'I believe a spell of prison is the very best way of keeping you apart, and you shall have it, or it will be no fault of mine.'

"'Oh, you would squeal, would you?' he cried, and in an instant he whipped out his revolver. I sprang for his hand, but saw that I was too late, and jumped aside. At the same instant he fired, and the bullet which would have struck me passed through the heart of my unfortunate brother.

"He dropped without a groan upon the floor of the compartment, and MacCoy and I, equally horrified, knelt at each side of him, trying to bring back some signs of life. MacCoy still held the loaded revolver in his hand, but his anger against me and my resentment towards him had both for the moment been swallowed up in this sudden tragedy. It was he who first realized the situation. The train was for some reason going very slowly at the moment, and he saw his opportunity for escape. In an instant he had the door open, but I was as quick as he, and jumping upon him the two of us fell off the foot-board and rolled in each other's arms down a steep embankment. At the bottom I struck my head against a stone, and I remembered nothing more. When I came to myself I was lying among some low bushes, not far from the railroad track, and somebody was bathing my head with a wet handkerchief. It was Sparrow MacCoy.

"'I guess I couldn't leave you,' said he. 'I didn't want to have the blood of two of you on my hands in one day. You loved your brother, I've no doubt; but you didn't love him a cent more than I loved him, though you'll say that I took a queer way to show it. Anyhow, it seems a mighty empty world now that he is gone, and I don't care a continental whether you give me over to the hangman or not.'

"He had turned his ankle in the fall, and there we sat, he with his useless foot, and I with my throbbing head, and we talked and talked until gradually my bitterness began to soften and to turn into something like sympathy. What was the use of revenging his death upon a man who was as much stricken by that death as I was? And then, as my wits gradually returned, I began to realize also that I could do nothing against MacCoy which would not recoil upon my mother and myself. How could we convict him without a full account of my brother's career being made public—the very thing which of all others we wished to avoid? It was really as much our interest as his to cover the matter up, and from being an avenger of crime I found myself changed to a conspirator against Justice. The place in which we found ourselves was one of those pheasant preserves which are so common in the Old Country, and as we groped our way through it I found myself consulting the slayer of my brother as to how far it would be possible to hush it up.

"I soon realized from what he said that unless there were some papers of which we knew nothing in my brother's pockets, there was really no possible means by which the police could identify him or learn how he had got there. His ticket was in MacCoy's pocket, and so was the ticket for some baggage which they had left at the depot. Like most Americans, he had found it cheaper and easier to buy an outfit in London than to bring one from New York, so that all his linen and clothes were new and unmarked. The bag containing the dust cloak, which I had thrown out of the window, may have fallen among some bramble patch where it is still concealed, or may have been carried off by some tramp, or may have come into the possession of the police, who kept the incident to themselves. Anyhow, I have seen nothing about it in the London papers. As to the watches, they were a selection from those which had been intrusted to him for business purposes. It may have been for the same business purposes that he was taking them to Manchester, but—well, it's too late to enter into that.

"I don't blame the police for being at fault. I don't see how it could have been otherwise. There was just one little clew that they might have followed up, but it was a small one. I mean that small circular mirror which was found in my brother's pocket. It isn't a very common thing for a young man to carry about with him, is it? But a gambler might have told you what such a mirror may mean to a card sharper. If you sit back a little from the table, and lay the mirror, face upwards, upon your lap, you can see, as you deal, every card that you give to your adversary. It is not hard to say whether you see a man or raise him when you know his cards as well as your own. It was as much a part of a sharper's outfit as the elastic clip upon Sparrow MacCoy's arm. Taking that, in connection with the recent frauds at the hotels, the police might have got hold of one end of the string.

"I don't think there is much more for me to explain We got to a village called Amersham that night in the character of two gentlemen upon a walking tour, and afterwards we made our way quietly to London, whence MacCoy went on to Cairo and I returned to New York. My mother died six months afterwards, and I am glad to say that to the day of her death she never knew what happened. She was always under the delusion that Edward was earning an honest living in London, and I never had the heart to tell her the truth. He never wrote; but, then, he never did write at any time, so that made no difference. His name was the last upon her lips.

"There's just one other thing that I have to ask you, sir, and I should take it as a kind return for all this explanation, if you could do it for me. You remember that Testament that was picked up. I always carried it in my inside pocket, and it must have come out in my fall. I value it very highly, for it was the family book with my birth and my brother's marked by my father in the beginning of it. I wish you would apply at the proper place and have it sent to me. It can be of no possible value to any one else. If you address it to X, Bassano's Library, Broadway, New York, it is sure to come to hand."

/ The Black Doctor /

Bishop's Crossing is a small village lying ten miles in a south-westerly direction from Liverpool. Here in the early seventies there settled a doctor named Aloysius Lana. Nothing was known locally either of his antecedents or of the reasons which had prompted him to come to this Lancashire hamlet. Two facts only were certain about him: the one that he had gained his medical qualification with some distinction at Glasgow; the other that he came undoubtedly of a tropical race, and was so dark that he might almost have had a strain of the Indian in his composition. His predominant features were, however, European, and he possessed a stately courtesy and carriage which suggested a Spanish extraction. A swarthy skin, raven-black hair, and dark, sparkling eyes under a pair of heavily-tufted brows made a strange contrast to the flaxen or chestnut rustics of England, and the newcomer was soon known as "The Black Doctor of Bishop's Crossing." At first it was a term of ridicule and reproach; as the years went on it became a title of honour which was familiar to the whole countryside, and extended far beyond the narrow confines of the village.

For the newcomer proved himself to be a capable surgeon and an accomplished physician. The practice of that district had been in the hands of Edward Rowe, the son of Sir William Rowe, the Liverpool consultant, but he had not inherited the talents of his father, and Dr. Lana, with his advantages of presence and of manner, soon beat him out of the field. Dr. Lana's social success was as rapid as his professional. A remarkable surgical cure in the case of the Hon. James Lowry, the second son of Lord Belton, was the means of introducing him to county society, where he became a favourite through the charm of his conversation and the elegance of his manners. An absence of antecedents and of relatives is sometimes an aid rather than an impediment to social advancement, and the distinguished individuality of the handsome doctor was its own recommendation.

His patients had one fault—and one fault only—to find with him. He appeared to be a confirmed bachelor. This was the more remarkable since the house which he occupied was a large one, and it was known that his success in practice had enabled him to save considerable sums. At first the local matchmakers were continually coupling his name with one or other of the eligible ladies, but as years passed and Dr. Lana remained unmarried, it came to be generally understood that for some reason he must remain a bachelor. Some even went so far as to assert that he was already married, and that it was in order to escape the consequence of an early misalliance that he had buried himself at Bishop's Crossing. And then, just as the matchmakers had finally given him up in despair, his engagement was suddenly announced to Miss Frances Morton, of Leigh Hall.

Miss Morton was a young lady who was well known upon the countryside, her father, James Haldane Morton, having been the squire of Bishop's Crossing. Both her parents were, however, dead, and she lived with her only brother, Arthur Morton, who had inherited the family estate. In person Miss Morton was tall and stately, and she was famous for her quick, impetuous nature and for her strength of character. She met Dr. Lana at a garden-party, and a friendship, which quickly ripened into love, sprang up between them. Nothing could exceed their devotion to each other. There was some discrepancy in age, he being thirty-seven, and she twenty-four; but, save in that one respect, there was no possible objection to be found with the match. The engagement was in February, and it was arranged that the marriage should take place in August.

Upon the 3rd of June Dr. Lana received a letter from abroad. In a small village the postmaster is also in a position to be the gossip-master, and Mr. Bankley, of Bishop's Crossing, had many of the secrets of his neighbours in his possession. Of this particular letter he remarked only that it was in a curious envelope, that it was in a man's handwriting, that the postscript was Buenos Ayres, and the stamp of the Argentine Republic. It was the first letter which he had ever known Dr. Lana to have from abroad, and this was the reason why his attention was particularly called to it before he handed it to the local postman. It was delivered by the evening delivery of that date.

Next morning—that is, upon the 4th of June—Dr. Lana called upon Miss Morton, and a long interview followed, from which he was observed to return in a state of great agitation. Miss Morton remained in her room all that day, and her maid found her several times in tears. In the course of a week it was an open secret to the whole village that the engagement was at an end, that Dr. Lana had behaved shamefully to the young lady, and that Arthur Morton, her brother, was talking of horsewhipping him. In what particular respect the doctor had behaved badly was unknown—some surmised one thing and some another; but it was observed, and taken as the obvious sign of a guilty conscience, that he would go for miles round rather than pass the windows of Leigh Hall, and that he gave up attending morning service upon Sundays where he might have met the young lady. There was an advertisement also in the *Lancet* as to the sale of a practice which mentioned no names, but which was thought by some to refer to Bishop's Crossing, and to mean that Dr. Lana was thinking of abandoning the scene of his success. Such was the position of affairs when, upon the evening of Monday, June 21st, there came a fresh development which changed what had been a mere village scandal into a tragedy which arrested the attention of the whole nation. Some detail is necessary to cause the facts of that evening to present their full significance.

The sole occupants of the doctor's house were his housekeeper, an elderly and most respectable woman, named Martha Woods, and a young servant—Mary Pilling.

The coachman and the surgery-boy slept out. It was the custom of the doctor to sit at night in his study, which was next the surgery in the wing of the house which was farthest from the servants' quarters. This side of the house had a door of its own for the convenience of patients, so that it was possible for the doctor to admit and receive a visitor there without the knowledge of anyone. As a matter of fact, when patients came late it was quite usual for him to let them in and out by the surgery entrance, for the maid and the housekeeper were in the habit of retiring early.

On this particular night Martha Woods went into the doctor's study at half-past nine, and found him writing at his desk. She bade him good-night, sent the maid to bed, and then occupied herself until a quarter to eleven in household matters. It was striking eleven upon the hall clock when she went to her own room. She had been there about a quarter of an hour or twenty minutes when she heard a cry or call, which appeared to come from within the house. She waited some time, but it was not repeated. Much alarmed, for the sound was loud and urgent, she put on a dressing-gown, and ran at the top of her speed to the doctor's study.

"Who's there?" cried a voice, as she tapped at the door.

"I am here, sir—Mrs. Woods."

"I beg that you will leave me in peace. Go back to your room this instant!" cried the voice, which was, to the best of her belief, that of her master. The tone was so harsh and so unlike her master's usual manner, that she was surprised and hurt.

"I thought I heard you calling, sir," she explained, but no answer was given to her. Mrs. Woods looked at the clock as she returned to her room, and it was then half-past eleven.

At some period between eleven and twelve (she could not be positive as to the exact hour) a patient called upon the doctor and was unable to get any reply from him. This late visitor was Mrs. Madding, the wife of the village grocer who was dangerously ill of typhoid fever. Dr. Lana had asked her to look in the last thing and let him know how her husband was progressing. She observed that the light was burning in the study, but having knocked several times at the surgery door without response, she concluded that the doctor had been called out, and so returned home.

There is a short, winding drive with a lamp at the end of it leading down from the house to the road. As Mrs. Madding emerged from the gate a man was coming along the footpath. Thinking that it might be Dr. Lana returning from some professional visit, she waited for him, and was surprised to see that it was Mr. Arthur Morton, the young squire. In the light of the lamp she observed that his manner was excited, and that he carried in his hand a heavy hunting-crop. He was turning in at the gate when she addressed him.

"The doctor is not in, sir," said she.

"How do you know that?" he asked, harshly.

"I have been to the surgery door, sir."

"I see a light," said the young squire, looking up the drive. "That is in his study, is it not?"

"Yes, sir; but I am sure that he is out."

"Well, he must come in again," said young Morton, and passed through the gate while Mrs. Madding went upon her homeward way.

At three o'clock that morning her husband suffered a sharp relapse, and she was so alarmed by his symptoms that she determined to call the doctor without delay. As she passed through the gate she was surprised to see someone lurking among the laurel bushes It was certainly a man, and to the best of her belief Mr. Arthur Morton. Preoccupied with her own troubles, she gave no particular attention to the incident, but hurried on upon her errand.

When she reached the house she perceived to her surprise that the light was still burning in the study. She therefore tapped at the surgery door. There was no answer. She repeated the knocking several times without effect. It appeared to her to be unlikely that the doctor would either go to bed or go out leaving so brilliant a light behind him, and it struck Mrs. Madding that it was possible that he might have dropped asleep in his chair. She tapped at the study window, therefore, but without result. Then, finding that there was an opening between the curtain and the woodwork, she looked through

The small room was brilliantly lighted from a large lamp on the central table, which was littered with the doctor's books and instruments. No one was visible, nor did she see anything unusual, except that in the further shadow thrown by the table a dingy white glove was lying upon the carpet. And then suddenly, as her eyes became more accustomed to the light, a boot emerged from the other end of the shadow, and she realized, with a thrill of horror, that what she had taken to be a glove was the hand of a man, who was prostrate upon the floor. Understanding that something terrible had occurred, she rang at the front door, roused Mrs. Woods, the housekeeper, and the two women made their way into the study, having first dispatched the maidservant to the police-station

At the side of the table, away from the window, Dr. Lana was discovered stretched upon his back and quite dead. It was evident that he had been subjected to violence, for one of his eyes was blackened, and there were marks of bruises about his face and neck. A slight thickening and swelling of his features appeared to suggest that the cause of his death had been strangulation. He was dressed in his usual professional clothes, but wore cloth slippers, the soles of which were perfectly clean. The carpet was marked all over, especially on the side of the door, with traces of dirty boots, which were presumably left by the murderer. It was evident that someone had entered by the surgery door, had killed the doctor, and had then made his escape unseen. That the assailant was a man was certain, from the size of the footprints and from the nature of the injuries. But beyond that point the police found it very difficult to go.

There were no signs of robbery, and the doctor's gold watch was safe in his pocket. He kept a heavy cash-box in the room, and this was discovered to be locked but empty. Mrs. Woods had an impression that a large sum was usually kept there, but the doctor had paid a heavy corn bill in cash only that very day, and it was conjectured that it was to this and not to a robber that the emptiness of the box was due. One thing in the room was missing—but that one thing was suggestive. The portrait of Miss Morton, which had always stood upon the side-table, had been taken from its frame, and carried off. Mrs. Woods had observed it there when she waited upon her employer that evening, and now it was gone. On the other hand, there was picked up from the floor a green eye-patch, which the housekeeper could not remember to have seen before. Such a patch might, however, be in the possession of a doctor, and there was nothing to indicate that it was in any way connected with the crime.

Suspicion could only turn in one direction, and Arthur Morton, the young squire, was immediately arrested. The evidence against him was circumstantial, but damning. He was devoted to his sister, and it was shown that since the rupture between her and Dr. Lana he had been heard again and again to express himself in the most vindictive terms towards her former lover. He had, as stated, been seen somewhere about eleven o'clock entering the doctor's drive with a hunting-crop in his hand. He had then, according to the theory of the police, broken in upon the doctor, whose exclamation of fear or of anger had been loud enough to attract the attention of Mrs. Woods. When Mrs Woods descended, Dr. Lana had made up his mind to talk it over with his visitor, and had, therefore, sent his housekeeper back to her room. This conversation had lasted a long time, had become more and more fiery, and had ended by a personal struggle, in which the doctor lost his life. The fact, revealed by a *post-mortem,* that his heart was much diseased—an ailment quite unsuspected during his life—would make it possible that death might in his case ensue from injuries which would not be fatal to a healthy man. Arthur Morton had then removed his sister's photograph, and had made his way homeward, stepping aside into the laurel bushes to avoid Mrs. Madding at the gate. This was the theory of the prosecution. and the case which they presented was a formidable one.

On the other hand, there were some strong points for the defence. Morton was high-spirited and impetuous, like his sister, but he was respected and liked by everyone, and his frank and honest nature seemed to be incapable of such a crime. His own explanation was that he was anxious to have a conversation with Dr. Lana about some urgent family matters (from first to last he refused even to mention the name of his sister). He did not attempt to deny that this conversation would probably have been of an unpleasant nature. He had heard from a patient that the doctor was out, and he therefore waited until about three in the morning for his return, but as he had seen nothing of him up to that hour, he had given it up and had returned home. As to his death, he knew no more about it than the constable who arrested him. He had formerly been an intimate friend of the deceased man; but circumstances, which he would prefer not to mention, had brought about a change in his sentiments.

There were several facts which supported his innocence. It was certain that Dr. Lana was alive and in his
study at half-past eleven o'clock. Mrs. Woods was prepared to swear that it was at that hour that she had heard
his voice. The friends of the prisoner contended that it was
probable that at that time Dr. Lana was not alone. The sound
which had originally attracted the attention of the housekeeper, and her master's unusual impatience that she should
leave him in peace, seemed to point to that. If this were so,
then it appeared to be probable that he had met his end
between the moment when the housekeeper heard his voice
and the time when Mrs. Madding made her first call and
found it impossible to attract his attention. But if this were
the time of his death, then it was certain that Mr. Arthur
Morton could not be guilty, as it was *after* this that she had
met the young squire at the gate.

If this hypothesis were correct, and someone was with
Dr. Lana before Mrs. Madding met Mr. Arthur Morton,
then who was this someone, and what motives had he for
wishing evil to the doctor? It was universally admitted that
if the friends of the accused could throw light upon this,
they would have gone a long way towards establishing his
innocence. But in the meanwhile it was open to the public
to say—as they did say—that there was no proof that anyone had been there at all except the young squire; while,
on the other hand, there was ample proof that his motives
in going were of a sinister kind. When Mrs. Madding called,
the doctor might have retired to his room, or he might, as
she thought at the time, have gone out and returned after-

wards to find Mr. Arthur Morton waiting for him. Some of the supporters of the accused laid stress upon the fact that the photograph of his sister Frances, which had been removed from the doctor's room, had not been found in her brother's possession. This argument, however, did not count for much, as he had ample time before his arrest to burn it or to destroy it. As to the only positive evidence in the case—the muddy footmarks upon the floor—they were so blurred by the softness of the carpet that it was impossible to make any trustworthy deduction from them. The most that could be said was that their appearance was not inconsistent with the theory that they were made by the accused, and it was further shown that his boots were very muddy upon that night. There had been a heavy shower in the afternoon, and all boots were probably in the same condition.

Such is a bald statement of the singular and romantic series of events which centred public attention upon this Lancashire tragedy. The unknown origin of the doctor, his curious and distinguished personality, the position of the man who was accused of the murder, and the love affair which had preceded the crime, all combined to make the affair one of those dramas which absorb the whole interest of a nation. Throughout the three kingdoms men discussed the case of the Black Doctor of Bishop's Crossing, and many were the theories put forward to explain the facts; but it may safely be said that among them all there was not one which prepared the minds of the public for the extraordinary sequel, which caused so much excitement upon the first day of the trial, and came to a climax upon the second. The long files of the *Lancaster Weekly* with their report of the case lie before me as I write, but I must content myself with a synopsis of the case up to the point when, upon the evening of the first day, the evidence of Miss Frances Morton threw a singular light upon the case.

Mr. Porlock Carr, the counsel for the prosecution, had marshalled his facts with his usual skill, and as the day wore on, it became more and more evident how difficult was the task which Mr. Humphrey, who had been retained for the defence, had before him. Several witnesses were put up to swear to the intemperate expressions which the young squire had been heard to utter about the doctor, and the fiery manner in which he resented the alleged ill-treatment of his sister. Mrs. Madding repeated her evidence as to the visit which had been paid late at night by the prisoner to the deceased, and it was shown by another witness that the prisoner was aware that the doctor was in the habit of sitting up alone in this isolated wing of the house, and that he had chosen this very late hour to call because he knew that his victim would then be at his mercy. A servant at the squire's house was compelled to admit that he had heard his master return about three that morning, which corroborated Mrs. Madding's statement that she had seen him among the laurel bushes near the gate upon the occasion of her second visit. The muddy boots and an alleged similarity in the footprints were duly dwelt upon, and it was felt when the case for the prosecution had been presented that, however circumstantial it might be, it was none the less so complete and so convincing, that the fate of the prisoner was sealed, unless something quite unexpected should be discosed by the defense. It was three o'clock when the prosecution closed. At half-past four, when the Court rose, a new and unlooked-for development had occurred. I extract the incident, or part of it, from this journal which I have already mentioned, omitting the preliminary observations of the counsel.

"Considerable sensation was caused in the crowded court when the first witness called for the defence proved to be Miss Frances Morton, the sister of the prisoner. Our readers will remember that the young lady had been engaged to Dr. Lana, and that it was his anger over the sudden termination of this engagement which was thought to have driven her brother to the perpetration of this crime. Miss Morton had not, however, been directly implicated in the case in any way, either at the inquest or at the police-court proceedings, and her appearance as the leading witness for the defence came as a surprise upon the public.

Miss Frances Morton, who was a tall and handsome brunette, gave her evidence in a low but clear voice, though it was evident throughout that she was suffering from extreme emotion. She alluded to her engagement to the doctor, touched briefly upon its termination, which was due, she said, to personal matters connected with his family, and surprised the Court by asserting that she had always considered her brother's resentment to be unreasonable and intemperate. In answer to a direct question from her counsel, she replied that she did not feel that she had any grievance whatever against Dr. Lana, and that in her opinion he had acted in a perfectly honourable manner. Her brother, on an insufficient knowledge of the facts, had taken another view, and she was compelled to acknowledge that, in spite of her entreaties, he had uttered threats of personal violence against the doctor, and had, upon the evening of the tragedy, announced his intention of "having it out with him." She had done her best to bring him to a more reasonable frame of mind, but he was very headstrong where his emotions or prejudices were concerned.

Up to this point the young lady's evidence had appeared to make the case against the prisoner rather than in his favour. The questions of her counsel, however, soon put a very different light upon the matter, and disclosed an unexpected line of defence.

Mr. Humphrey: Do you believe your brother to be guilty of this crime?

The Judge: I cannot permit that question, Mr. Humphrey. We are here to decide upon questions of fact—not of belief.

Mr. Humphrey: Do you know that your brother is not guilty of the death of Doctor Lana?

Miss Morton: Yes.

Mr. Humphrey: How do you know it?

Miss Morton: Because Dr. Lana is not dead.

There followed a prolonged sensation in court, which interrupted the cross-examination of the witness.

Mr. Humphrey: And how do you know, Miss Morton, that Dr. Lana is not dead?

Miss Morton: Because I have received a letter from him since the date of his supposed death.

Mr. Humphrey: Have you this letter?

Miss Morton: Yes, but I should prefer not to show it.

Mr. Humphrey: Have you the envelope?

Miss Morton: Yes, it is here.

Mr. Humphrey: What is the post-mark?

Miss Morton: Liverpool.

Mr. Humphrey: And the date?

Miss Morton: June the 22nd.

Mr. Humphrey: That being the day after his alleged death. Are you prepared to swear to this handwriting, Miss Morton?

Miss Morton: Certainly.

Mr. Humphrey: I am prepared to call six other witnesses, my lord, to testify that this letter is in the writing of Doctor Lana.

The Judge: Then you must call them tomorrow.

Mr. Porlock Carr (counsel for the prosecution): In the meantime, my lord, we claim possession of this document, so that we may obtain expert evidence as to how far it is an imitation of the handwriting of the gentleman whom we still confidently assert to be deceased. I need not point out that the theory so unexpectedly sprung upon us may prove to be a very obvious device adopted by the friends of the prisoner in order to divert this inquiry. I would draw attention to the fact that the young lady must, according to her own account, have possessed this letter during the proceedings at the inquest and at the police-court. She desires us to believe that she permitted these to proceed, although she held in her pocket evidence which would at any moment have brought them to an end.

Mr. Humphrey: Can you explain this, Miss Morton?

Miss Morton: Dr. Lana desired his secret to be preserved.

Mr. Porlock Carr: Then why have you made this public?

Miss Morton: To save my brother.

A murmur of sympathy broke out in court, which was instantly suppressed by the Judge.

The Judge: Admitting this line of defence, it lies with you, Mr. Humphrey, to throw a light upon who this man is whose body has been recognised by so many friends and patients of Dr. Lana as being that of the doctor himself.

A Juryman: Has anyone up to now expressed any doubt about the matter?

Mr. Porlock Carr: Not to my knowledge.

Mr. Humphrey: We hope to make the matter clear.

The Judge: Then the Court adjourns until tomorrow."

This new development of the case excited the utmost interest among the general public. Press comment was prevented by the fact that the trial was still undecided, but the question was everywhere argued as to how far there could be truth in Miss Morton's declaration, and how far it might be a daring ruse for the purpose of saving her brother. The obvious dilemma in which the missing doctor stood was that if by any extraordinary chance he was not dead, then he must be held responsible for the death of this unknown man, who resembled him so exactly, and who was found in his study. This letter which Miss Morton refused to produce was possibly a confession of guilt, and she might find herself in the terrible position of only being able to save her brother from the gallows by the sacrifice of her former lover. The court next morning was crammed to overflowing, and a murmur of excitement passed over it when Mr. Humphrey was observed to enter in a state of emotion, which even his trained nerves could not conceal, and to confer with the opposing counsel. A few hurried words—words which left a look of amazement upon Mr. Porlock Carr's face—passed between them, and then the counsel for the defence, addressing the judge, announced that, with the consent of the prosecution, the young lady who had already given evidence would not be recalled.

The Judge: But you appear, Mr. Humphrey, to have left matters in a very unsatisfactory state.

Mr. Humphrey: Perhaps, my lord, my next witness may help to clear them up.

The Judge: Then call your next witness.

Mr. Humphrey: I call Dr. Aloysius Lana.

The learned counsel has made many telling remarks in his day, but he has certainly never produced such a sensation with so short a sentence. The Court was simply stunned with amazement as the very man whose fate had been the subject of so much contention appeared bodily before them in the witness-box. Those among the spectators who had known him at Bishop's Crossing saw him now, gaunt and thin, with deep lines of care upon his face. But in spite of his melancholy bearing and despondent expression, there were few who could say that they had ever seen a man of more distinguished presence. Bowing to the judge, he asked if he might be allowed to make a statement, and having been duly informed that whatever he said might be used against him, he bowed once more, and proceeded:—

"My wish," said he, "is to hold nothing back, but to tell with perfect frankness all that occurred upon the night of the 21st of June. Had I known that the innocent had suffered, and that so much trouble had been brought upon those whom I love best in the world, I should have come forward long ago; but there were reasons which prevented these things from coming to my ears. It was my desire that an unhappy man should vanish from the world which had known him, but I had not foreseen that others would be affected by my actions. Let me to the best of my ability repair the evil which I have done.

"To any one who is acquainted with the history of the Argentine Republic the name of Lana is well known. My father, who came of the best blood of old Spain, filled all the highest offices of the State, and would have been President but for his death in the riots of San Juan. A brilliant career might have been open to my twin brother Ernest and myself had it not been for financial losses which made it necessary that we should earn our own living. I apologize, sir, if these details appear to be irrelevant, but they are a necessary introduction to that which is to follow.

"I had, as I have said, a twin brother named Ernest, whose resemblance to me was so great that even when we were together people could see no difference between us. Down to the smallest detail we were exactly the same. As we grew older this likeness became less marked because our expression was not the same, but with our features in repose the points of difference were very slight.

"It does not become me to say too much of one who is dead, the more so as he is my only brother, but I leave his character to those who knew him best. I will only say— for I *have* to say it—that in my early manhood I conceived a horror of him, and that I had good reason for the aversion which filled me. My own reputation suffered from his actions, for our close resemblance caused me to be credited with many of them, Eventually, in a peculiarly disgraceful business, he contrived to throw the whole odium upon me in such a way that I was forced to leave the Argentine for ever, and to seek a career in Europe. The freedom from his hated presence more than compensated me for the loss of my native land. I had enough money to defray my medical studies at Glasgow, and I finally settled in practice at Bishop's Crossing, in the firm conviction that in that remote Lancashire hamlet I should never hear of him again.

"For years my hopes were fulfilled, and then at last he discovered me. Some Liverpool man who visited Buenos Ayres put him upon my track. He had lost all his money, and he thought that he would come over and share mine. Knowing my horror of him, he rightly thought that I would be willing to buy him off. I received a letter from him saying that he was coming. It was at a crisis in my own affairs, and his arrival might conceivably bring trouble, and even disgrace, upon some whom I was especially bound to shield from anything of the kind. I took steps to insure that any evil which might come should fall on me only, and that"—here he turned and looked at the prisoner—"was the cause of conduct upon my part which has been too harshly judged. My only motive was to screen those who were dear to me from any possible connection with scandal or disgrace. That scandal and disgrace would come with my brother was only to say that what had been would be again.

"My brother arrived himself one night not very long after my receipt of the letter. I was sitting in my study after the servants had gone to bed, when I heard a footstep upon the gravel outside, and an instant later I saw his face looking in at me through the window. He was a clean-shaven man like myself, and the resemblance between us was still so great that, for an instant, I thought it was my own reflection in the glass. He had a dark patch over his eye, but our features were absolutely the same. Then he smiled in a sardonic way which had been a trick of his from his boyhood, and I knew that he was the same brother who had driven me from my native land, and brought disgrace upon what had been an honourable name. I went to the door and I admitted him. That would be about ten o'clock that night.

"When he came into the glare of the lamp, I saw at once that he had fallen upon very evil days. He had walked from Liverpool, and he was tired and ill. I was quite shocked by the expression upon his face. My medical knowledge told me that there was some serious internal malady. He had been drinking also, and his face was bruised as the result of a scuffle which he had had with some sailors. It was to cover his injured eye that he wore this patch, which he removed when he entered the room. He was himself dressed in a peajacket and flannel shirt, and his feet were bursting through his boots. But his poverty had only made him more savagely vindictive towards me. His hatred rose to the height of a mania. I had been rolling in money in England, according to his account, while he had been starving in South America. I cannot describe to you the threats which he uttered or the insults which he poured upon me. My impression is, that hardships and debauchery had unhinged his reason. He paced about the room like a wild beast, demanding drink, demanding money, and all in the foulest language. I am a hot-tempered man, but I thank God that I am able to say that I remained master of myself, and that I never raised a hand against him. My coolness only irritated him the more. He raved, he cursed, he shook his fists in my face, and then suddenly a horrible spasm passed over his features, he clapped his hand to his side, and with a loud cry he fell in a heap at my feet. I raised him up and stretched him upon the sofa, but no answer came to my exclamations, and the hand which I held in mine was cold and clammy. His diseased heart had broken down. His own violence had killed him.

"For a long time I sat as if I were in some dreadful dream, staring at the body of my brother. I was aroused by the knocking of Mrs. Woods, who had been disturbed by that dying cry. I sent her away to bed. Shortly afterwards a patient tapped at the surgery door, but as I took no notice, he or she went off again. Slowly and gradually as I sat there a plan was forming itself in my head in the curious automatic way in which plans do form. When I rose from my chair my future movements were finally decided upon without my having been conscious of any process of thought. It was an instinct which irresistibly inclined me towards one course.

"Ever since that change in my affairs to which I have alluded, Bishop's Crossing had become hateful to me. My plans of life had been ruined, and I had met with hasty judgments and unkind treatment where I had expected sympathy. It is true that any danger of scandal from my brother had passed away with his life; but still, I was sore about the past, and felt that things could never be as they had been. It may be that I was unduly sensitive, and that I had not made sufficient allowance for others, but my feelings were as I describe. Any chance of getting away from Bishop's Crossing and of everyone in it would be most welcome to me. And here was such a chance as I could never have dared to hope for, a chance which would enable me to make a clean break with the past.

"There was this dead man lying upon the sofa, so like me that save for some little thickness and coarseness of the features there was no difference at all. No one had seen him come and no one would miss him. We were both clean shaven, and his hair was about the same length as my own. If I changed clothes with him, then Dr. Aloysius Lana would be found lying dead in his study, and there would be an end of an unfortunate fellow, and of a blighted career. There was plenty of ready money in the room, and this I could carry away with me to help me to start once more in some other land. In my brother's clothes I could walk by night unobserved as far as Liverpool, and in that great seaport I would soon find some means of leaving the country. After my lost hopes, the humblest existence where I was unknown was far preferable, in my estimation, to a practice, however successful, in Bishop's Crossing, where at any moment I might come face to face with those whom I should wish, if it were possible, to forget. I determined to effect the change.

"And I did so. I will not go into particulars, for the recollection is as painful as the experience; but in an hour my brother lay, dressed down to the smallest detail in my clothes, while I slunk out by the surgery door, and taking the back path which led across some fields, I started off to make the best of my way to Liverpool, where I arrived the same night. My bag of money and a certain portrait were all I carried out of the house, and I left behind me in my hurry the shade which my brother had been wearing over his eye. Everything else of his I took with me.

"I give you my word, sir, that never for one instant did the idea occur to me that people might think that I had been murdered, nor did I imagine that anyone might be caused serious danger through this stratagem by which I endeavoured to gain a fresh start in the world. On the contrary, it was the thought of relieving others from the burden of my presence which was always uppermost in my mind. A sailing vessel was leaving Liverpool that very day for Corunna, and in this I took my passage, thinking that the voyage would give me time to recover my balance, and to consider the future. But before I left my resolution softened. I bethought me that there was one person in the world to whom I would not cause an hour of sadness. She would mourn me in her heart, however harsh and unsympathetic her relatives might be. She understood and appreciated the motives upon which I had acted, and if the rest of her family condemned me, she, at least, would not forget. And so I sent her a note under the seal of secrecy to save her from a baseless grief. If under the pressure of events she broke that seal, she has my entire sympathy and forgiveness.

"It was only last night that I returned to England, and during all this time I have heard nothing of the sensation which my supposed death had caused, nor of the accusation that Mr. Arthur Morton had been concerned in it. It was in a late evening paper that I read an account of the proceedings of yesterday, and I have come this morning as fast as an express train could bring me to testify to the truth."

Such was the remarkable statement of Dr. Aloysius Lana which brought the trial to a sudden termination. A subsequent investigation corroborated it to the extent of finding out the vessel in which his brother Ernest Lana had come over from South America. The ship's doctor was able to testify that he had complained of a weak heart during the voyage, and that his symptoms were consistent with such a death as was described.

As to Dr. Aloysius Lana, he returned to the village from which he had made so dramatic a disappearance, and a complete reconciliation was effected between him and the young squire, the latter having acknowledged that he had entirely misunderstood the other's motives in withdrawing from his engagement. That another reconciliation followed may be judged from a notice extracted from a prominent column in the *Morning Post:*—

A marriage was solemnized upon September 19th, by the Rev. Stephen Johnson, at the parish church of Bishop's Crossing, between Aloysius Xavier Lana, son of Don Alfredo Lana, formerly Foreign Minister of the Argentine republic, and Frances Morton, only daughter of the late James Morton, Jr., of Leigh Hall, Bishop's Crossing, Lancashire.

/ The Jew's Breastplate /

My particular friend Ward Mortimer was one of the best men of his day at everything connected with Oriental archaeology. He had written largely upon the subject, he had lived two years in a tomb at Thebes, while he excavated in the Valley of the Kings, and finally he had created a considerable sensation by his exhumation of the alleged mummy of Cleopatra in the inner room of the Temple of Horus, at Philae. With such a record at the age of thirty-one, it was felt that a considerable career lay before him, and no one was surprised when he was elected to the curatorship of the Belmore Street Museum, which carries with it the lectureship at the Oriental College, and an income which has sunk with the fall in land, but which still remains at that ideal sum which is large enough to encourage an investigator, but not so large as to enervate him.

There was only one reason which made Ward Mortimer's position a little difficult at the Belmore Street Museum, and that was the extreme eminence of the man whom he had to succeed. Professor Andreas was a profound scholar and a man of European reputation. His lectures were frequented by students from every part of the world, and his admirable management of the collection intrusted to his care was a commonplace in all learned societies. There was, therefore, considerable surprise when, at the age of fifty-five, he suddenly resigned his position and retired from those duties which had been both his livelihood and his pleasure. He and his daughter left the comfortable suite of rooms which had formed his official residence in connection with the museum, and my friend, Mortimer, who was a bachelor, took up his quarters there.

On hearing of Mortimer's appointment, Professor Andreas had written him a very kindly and flattering congratulatory letter. I was actually present at their first meeting, and I went with Mortimer round the museum when the Professor showed us the admirable collection which he had cherished so long. The professor's beautiful daughter and a young man, Captain Wilson, who was, as I understood, soon to be her husband, accompanied us in our inspection. There were fifteen rooms, but the Babylonian, the Syrian, and the central hall, which contained the Jewish and Egyptian collection, were the finest of all. Professor Andreas was a quiet, dry, elderly man, with a clean-shaven face and an impassive manner, but his dark eyes sparkled and his features quickened into enthusiastic life as he pointed out to us the rarity and the beauty of some of his specimens. His hand lingered so fondly over them, that one could read his pride in them and the grief in his heart now that they were passing from his care into that of another.

He had shown us in turn his mummies, his papyri, his rare scarabs, his inscriptions, his Jewish relics, and his duplication of the famous seven-branched candlestick of the Temple, which was brought to Rome by Titus, and which is supposed by some to be lying at this instant in the bed of the Tiber. Then he approached a case which stood in the very centre of the hall, and he looked down through the glass with reverence in his attitude and manner.

"This is no novelty to an expert like yourself, Mr. Mortimer," said he; "but I daresay that your friend, Mr. Jackson, will be interested to see it."

Leaning over the case I saw an object, some five inches square, which consisted of twelve precious stones in a framework of gold, with golden hooks at two of the corners. The stones were all varying in sort and colour, but they were of the same size. Their shapes, arrangement, and gradation of tint made me think of a box of water-colour paints. Each stone had some hieroglyphic scratched upon its surface.

"You have heard, Mr Jackson, of the urim and thummim?"

I had heard the term, but my idea of its meaning was exceedingly vague.

"The urim and thummim was a name given to the jew-elled plate which lay upon the breast of the high priest of the Jews. They had a very special feeling of reverence for it—something of the feeling which an ancient Roman might have for the Sibylline books in the Capitol. There are, as you see, twelve magnificent stones, inscribed with mystical characters. Counting from the left-hand top corner, the stones are carnelian, peridot, emerald, ruby, lapis lazuli, onyx, sapphire, agate, amethyst, topaz, beryl, and jasper."

I was amazed at the variety and beauty of the stones.

"Has the breastplate any particular history?" I asked.

"It is of great age and of immense value," said Professor Andreas. "Without being able to make an absolute assertion, we have many reasons to think that it is possible that it may be the original urim and thummim of Solomon's Temple. There is certainly nothing so fine in any collection in Europe. My friend, Captain Wilson here, is a practiced authority upon precious stones, and he would tell you how pure these are."

Captain Wilson, a man with a dark, hard, incisive face, was standing beside his fiancée at the other side of the case.

"Yes," said he, curtly, "I have never seen finer stones."

"And the gold-work is also worthy of attention. The ancients excelled in"—he was apparently about to indicate the setting of the stones, when Captain Wilson interrupted him.

"You will see a finer example of their gold-work in this candlestick," said he, turning to another table, and we all joined him in his admiration of its embossed stem and delicately ornamented branches. Altogether it was an interesting and a novel experience to have objects of such rarity explained by so great an expert; and when, finally, Professor Andreas finished our inspection by formally handing over the precious collection to the care of my friend, I could not help pitying him and envying his successor whose life was to pass in so pleasant a duty. Within a week, Ward Mortimer was duly installed in his new set of rooms, and had become the autocrat of the Belmore Street Museum.

About a fortnight afterwards my friend gave a small dinner to half-a-dozen bachelor friends to celebrate his promotion. When his guests were departing he pulled my sleeve and signalled to me that he wished me to remain.

"You have only a few hundred yards to go," said he—I was living in chambers in the Albany. "You may as well stay and have a quiet cigar with me. I very much want your advice."

I relapsed into an armchair and lit one of his excellent Matronas. When he had returned from seeing the last of his guests out, he drew a letter from his dress-jacket and sat down opposite to me.

"This is an anonymous letter which I received this morning," said he. "I want to read it to you and to have your advice."

"You are very welcome to it for what it is worth."

"This is how the note runs: 'Sir,—I should strongly advise you to keep a very careful watch over the many valuable things which are committed to your charge. I do not think that the present system of a single watchman is sufficient. Be upon your guard, or an irreparable misfortune may occur.'"

"Is that all?"

"Yes, that is all."

"Well," said I, "it is at least obvious that it was written by one of the limited number of people who are aware that you have only one watchman at night."

Ward Mortimer handed me the note, with a curious smile. "Have you an eye for handwriting?" said he. "Now, look at this!" He put another letter in front of me. "Look at the c in 'congratulate' and the c in 'committed.' Look at the capital I. Look at the trick of putting in a dash instead of a stop!"

"They are undoubtedly from the same hand—with some attempt at disguise in the case of this first one."

"The second," said Ward Mortimer, "is the letter of congratulation which was written to me by Professor Andreas upon my obtaining my appointment."

I stared at him in amazement. Then I turned over the letter in my hand, and there, sure enough, was "Martin Andreas" signed upon the other side. There could be no doubt, in the mind of any one who had the slightest knowledge of the science of graphology, that the Professor had written an anonymous letter, warning his successor against thieves. It was inexplicable, but it was certain.

"Why should he do it?" I asked.

"Precisely what I should wish to ask you. If he had any such misgivings, why could he not come and tell me direct?"

"Will you speak to him about it?"

"There again I am in doubt. He might choose to deny that he wrote it."

"At any rate," said I, "this warning is meant in a friendly spirit, and I should certainly act upon it. Are the present precautions enough to insure you against robbery?"

"I should have thought so. The public are only admitted from ten till five, and there is one guardian to every two rooms. He stands at the door between them, and so commands them both."

"But at night?"

"When the public are gone, we at once put up the great iron shutters, which are absolutely burglar-proof. The watchman is a capable fellow. He sits in the lodge, but he walks round every three hours. We keep one electric light burning in each room all night."

"It is difficult to suggest anything more—short of keeping your day watchers all night."

"We could not afford that."

"At least, I should communicate with the police, and have a special constable put on outside in Belmore Street," said I. "As to the letter, if the writer wishes to be anonymous, I think he has a right to remain so. We must trust to the future to show some reason for the curious course which he has adopted."

So we dismissed the subject, but all that night after my return to my chambers I was puzzling my brain as to what possible motive Professor Andreas could have for writing an anonymous warning letter to his successor—for that the writing was his was as certain to me as if I had seen him actually doing it. He foresaw some danger to the collection. Was it because he foresaw it that he abandoned his charge of it? But if so, why should he hesitate to warn Mortimer in his own name? I puzzled and puzzled until at last I fell into a troubled sleep, which carried me beyond my usual hour of rising.

I was aroused in a singular and effective method, for about nine o'clock my friend Mortimer rushed into my room with an expression of consternation upon his face. He was usually one of the most tidy men of my acquaintance, but now his collar was undone at one end, his tie was flying, and his hat at the back of his head. I read his whole story in his frantic eyes.

"The museum has been robbed!" I cried, springing up in bed.

"I fear so! Those jewels! The jewels of the urim and thummim!" he gasped, for he was out of breath with running. "I'm going on to the police-station. Come to the museum as soon as you can, Jackson! Good-bye!" He rushed distractedly out of the room, and I heard him clatter down the stairs.

I was not long in following his directions, but I found when I arrived that he had already returned with a police inspector, and another elderly gentleman, who proved to be Mr. Purvis, one of the partners of Morson and Company, the well-known diamond merchants. As an expert in stones he was always prepared to advise the police. They were grouped round the case in which the breastplate of the Jewish priest had been exposed. The plate had been taken out and laid upon the glass top of the case, and the three heads were bent over it.

"It is obvious that it has been tampered with," said Mortimer. "It caught my eye the moment that I passed through the room this morning. I examined it yesterday evening, so that it is certain that this has happened during the night."

It was, as he had said, obvious that someone had been at work upon it. The settings of the uppermost row of four stones—the carnelian, peridot, emerald, and ruby—were rough and jagged as if some one had scraped all round them. The stones were in their places, but the beautiful goldwork which we had admired only a few days before had been very clumsily pulled about.

"It looks to me," said the police inspector, "as if some one had been trying to take out the stone."

"My fear is," said Mortimer, "that he not only tried, but succeeded. I believe these four stones to be skilful imitations which have been put in the place of the originals."

The same suspicion had evidently been in the mind of the expert, for he had been carefully examining the four stones with the aid of a lens. He now submitted them to several tests, and finally turned cheerfully to Mortimer.

"I congratulate you, sir," said he, heartily. "I will pledge my reputation that all four of these stones are genuine, and of a most unusual degree of purity."

The colour began to come back to my poor friend's frightened face, and he drew a long breath of relief.

"Thank God!" he cried. "Then what in the world did the thief want?"

"Probably he meant to take the stones, but was interrupted."

"In that case one would expect him to take them out one at a time, but the setting of each of these has been loosened, and yet the stones are all here."

"It is certainly most extraordinary," said the inspector. "I never remember a case like it. Let us see the watchman."

The commissionaire was called—a soldierly, honest-faced man, who seemed as concerned as Ward Mortimer at the incident.

"No, sir, I never heard a sound," he answered, in reply to the questions of the inspector. "I made my rounds four times, as usual, but I saw nothing suspicious. I've been in my position ten years, but nothing of the kind has ever occurred before."

"No thief could have come through the windows?"

"Impossible, sir."

"Or passed you at the door?"

"No, sir; I never left my post except when I walked my rounds."

"What other openings are there in the museum?"

"There is the door into Mr. Ward Mortimer's private rooms."

"That is locked at night," my friend explained, "and in order to reach it anyone from the street would have to open the outside door as well."

"Your servants?"

"Their quarters are entirely separate."

"Well, well," said the inspector, "this is certainly very obscure. However, there has been no harm done, according to Mr. Purvis."

"I will swear that those stones are genuine."

"So that the case appears to be merely one of malicious damage. But none the less, I should be very glad to go carefully round the premises, and to see if we can find any trace to show us who your visitor may have been."

His investigation, which lasted all the morning, was careful and intelligent, but it led in the end to nothing. He pointed out to us that there were two possible entrances to the museum which we had not considered. The one was from the cellars, by a trap-door opening in the passage. The other through a skylight from the lumber-room, overlooking that very chamber to which the intruder had penetrated. As neither the cellar nor the lumber-room could be entered unless the thief was already within the locked doors, the matter was not of any practical importance, and the dust of cellar and attic assured us that no one had used either one or the other. Finally, we ended as we began, without the slightest clue as to how, why, or by whom the setting of these four jewels had been tampered with.

There remained one course for Mortimer to take, and he took it. Leaving the police to continue their fruitless researches, he asked me to accompany him that afternoon in a visit to Professor Andreas. He took with him the two letters, and it was his intention to openly tax his predecessor with having written the anonymous warning, and to ask him to explain the fact that he should have anticipated so exactly that which had actually occurred. The Professor was living in a small villa in Upper Norwood, but we were informed by the servant that he was away from home. Seeing our disappointment, she asked us if we should like to see Miss Andreas, and showed us into the modest drawing room.

I have mentioned incidentally that the Professor's daughter was a very beautiful girl. She was a blonde, tall, and graceful, with a skin of that delicate tint which the French call "mat," the colour of old ivory or of the lighter petals of the sulphur rose. I was shocked, however, as she entered the room to see how much she had changed in the last fortnight. Her young face was haggard and her bright eyes heavy with trouble.

"Father has gone to Scotland," she said. "He seems to be tired, and has had a good deal to worry him. He only left us yesterday."

"You look a little tired yourself, Miss Andreas," said my friend.

"I have been so anxious about father."

"Can you give me his Scotch address?"

"Yes, he is with his brother, the Rev. David Andreas, 1, Arran Villas, Ardrossan."

Ward Mortimer made a note of the address, and we left without saying anything as to the objects of our visit. We found ourselves in Belmore Street in the evening in exactly the same position in which we had been in the morning. Our only clue was the Professor's letter, and my friend had made up his mind to start for Ardrossan next day, and to get to the bottom of the anonymous letter, when a new development came to alter our plans.

Very early on the following morning I was aroused from my sleep by a tap upon my bedroom door. It was a messenger with a note from Mortimer.

"Do come round," it said; "the matter is becoming more and more extraordinary."

When I obeyed his summons I found him pacing excitedly up and down the central room, while the old soldier who guarded the premises stood with military stiffness in a corner.

"My dear Jackson," he cried, "I am so delighted that you have come, for this is a most inexplicable business."

"What has happened, then?"

He waved his hand towards the case which contained the breastplate.

"Look at it," said he.

I did so, and could not restrain a cry of surprise. The setting of the middle row of precious stones had been profaned in the same manner as the upper ones. Of the twelve jewels, eight had been now tampered with in this singular fashion. The setting of the lower four was neat and smooth. The others jagged and irregular.

"Have the stones been altered?" I asked.

"No, I am certain that these upper four are the same which the expert pronounced to be genuine, for I observed yesterday that little discoloration on the edge of the emerald. Since they have not extracted the upper stones, there is no reason to think the lower have been transposed. You say that you heard nothing, Simpson?"

"No, sir," the commissionaire answered. "But when I made my round after daylight I had a special look at these stones, and I saw at once that someone had been meddling with them. Then I called you, sir, and told you. I was backwards and forwards all the night, and I never saw a soul or heard a sound."

"Come up and have some breakfast with me," said Mortimer, and he took me into his own chambers. "Now, what *do* you think of this, Jackson?" he asked.

"It is the most objectless, futile, idiotic business that ever I heard of. It can only be the work of a monomaniac."

"Can you put forward any theory?"

A curious idea came into my head. "This object is a Jewish relic of great antiquity and sanctity," said I. "How about the anti-Semitic movement? Could one conceive that a fanatic of that way of thinking might desecrate—"

"No, no, no!" cried Mortimer. "That will never do! Such a man might push his lunacy to the length of destroying a Jewish relic, but why on earth should he nibble round every stone so carefully that he can only do four stones in a night? We must have a better solution than that, and we must find it for ourselves, for I do not think that our inspector is likely to help us. First of all, what do you think of Simpson, the porter?"

"Have you any reason to suspect him?"

"Only that he is the one person on the premises."

"But why should he indulge in such wanton destruction? Nothing has been taken away. He has no motive."

"Mania?"

"No, I will swear to his sanity."

"Have you any other theory?"

"Well, yourself, for example. You are not a somnambulist, by any chance?"

"Nothing of the sort, I assure you."

"Then I give it up."

"But I don't—and I have a plan by which we will make it all clear,"

"To visit Professor Andreas?"

"No, we shall find our solution nearer than Scotland. I will tell you what we shall do. You know that skylight which overlooks the central hall? We will leave the electric lights in the hall, and we will keep watch in the lumber-room, you and I, and solve the mystery for ourselves. If our mysterious visitor is doing four stones at a time, he has four still to do, and there is every reason to think that he will return tonight and complete the job,"

"Excellent!" I cried.

"We will keep our own secret, and say nothing, either to the police or to Simpson. Will you join me?"

"With the utmost pleasure," said I; and so it was agreed,

It was ten o'clock that night when I returned to the Belmore Street Museum. Mortimer was, as I could see, in a state of suppressed nervous excitement, but it was still too early to begin our vigil, so we remained for an hour or so in his chambers, discussing all the possibilities of the singular business which we had met to solve. At last the roaring stream of hansom cabs and the rush of hurrying feet became lower and more intermittent as the pleasure-seekers passed on their way to their stations or their homes. It was nearly twelve when Mortimer led the way to the lumber-room which overlooked the central hall of the museum.

He had visited it during the day, and had spread some sacking so that we could lie at our ease, and look straight down into the museum. The skylight was of unfrosted glass, but was so covered with dust that it would be impossible for anyone looking up from below to detect that he was overlooked. We cleared a small piece at each corner, which gave us a complete view of the room beneath us. In the cold white light of the electric lamps everything stood out hard and clear, and I could see the smallest detail of the contents of the various cases.

Such a vigil is an excellent lesson, since one has no choice but to look hard at those objects which we usually pass with such half-hearted interest. Through my little peep-hole I employed the hours in studying every specimen, from the huge mummy-case which leaned against the wall to those very jewels which had brought us there, gleaming and sparkling in their glass case immediately beneath us. There was much precious gold-work and many valuable stones scattered through the numerous cases, but those wonderful twelve which made up the urim and thummim glowed and burned with a radiance which far eclipsed the others. I studied in turn the tomb-pictures of Sicara, the friezes from Karnak, the statues of Memphis, and the inscriptions of Thebes, but my eyes would always come back to that wonderful Jewish relic, and my mind to the singular mystery which surrounded it. I was lost in the thought of it when my companion suddenly drew his breath sharply in, and seized my arm in a convulsive grip. At the same instant I saw what it was which had excited him.

I have said that against the wall—on the right hand side of the doorway (the right-hand side as we looked at it, but the left as one entered)—there stood a large mummy-case. To our unutterable amazement it was slowly opening. Gradually, gradually the lid was swinging back, and the black slit which marked the opening was becoming wider and wider. So gently and carefully was it done that the movement was almost imperceptible. Then, as we breathlessly watched it, a white thin hand appeared at the opening, pushing back the painted lid, then another hand, and finally a face—a face which was familiar to us both, that of Professor Andreas. Stealthily he slunk out of the mummy-case, like a fox stealing from its burrow, his head turning incessantly to left and to right, stepping, then pausing, then stepping again, the very image of craft and of caution. Once some sound in the street struck him motionless, and he stood listening, with his ear turned, ready to dart back to the shelter behind him. Then he crept onwards again upon tiptoe, very, very softly and slowly, until he had reached the case in the centre of the room. There he took a bunch of keys from his pocket, unlocked the case, took out the Jewish breastplate, and, laying it upon the glass in front of him, began to work upon it with some sort of small, glistening tool. He was so directly underneath us that his bent head covered his work, but we could guess

from the movement of his hand that he was engaged in
finishing the strange disfigurement which he had begun.

I could realize from the heavy breathing of my companion, and the twitching of the hand which still clutched
my wrist, the furious indignation which filled his heart as
he saw this vandalism in the quarter of all others where he
could least have expected it. He, the very man who a fortnight before had reverently bent over this unique relic, and
who had impressed its antiquity and its sanctity upon us,
was now engaged in this outrageous profanation. It was
impossible, unthinkable—and yet there, in the white glare
of the electric light beneath us, was that dark figure with
the bent, grey head, and the twitching elbow. What inhuman hypocrisy, what hateful depth of malice against his
successor must underlie these sinister nocturnal labours.
It was painful to think of and dreadful to watch. Even I,
who had none of the acute feelings of a virtuoso, could not
bear to look on and see this deliberate mutilation of so
ancient a relic. It was a relief to me when my companion
tugged at my sleeve as a signal that I was to follow him as
he softly crept out of the room. It was not until we were
within his own quarters that he opened his lips, and then I
saw by his agitated face how deep was his consternation.

"The abominable Goth!" he cried. "Could you have
believed it?"

"It is amazing."

"He is a villain or a lunatic—one or the other. We shall
very soon see which. Come with me, Jackson, and we shall
get to the bottom of this black business."

A door opened out of the passage which was the private entrance from his rooms into the museum. This he opened softly with his key, having first kicked off his shoes, an example which I followed. We crept together through room after room, until the large hall lay before us, with that dark figure still stooping and working at the central case. With an advance as cautious as his own we closed in upon him, but softly as we went we could not take him entirely unawares. We were still a dozen yards from him when he looked round with a start, and uttering a husky cry of terror, ran frantically down the museum.

"Simpson! Simpson!" roared Mortimer, and far away down the vista of electric lighted doors we saw the stiff figure of the old soldier suddenly appear. Professor Andreas saw him also, and stopped running, with a gesture of despair. At the same instant we each laid a hand upon his shoulder.

"Yes, yes, gentlemen," he panted, "I will come with you. To your room, Mr. Ward Mortimer, if you please! I feel that I owe you an explanation."

My companion's indignation was so great that I could see that he dared not trust himself to reply. We walked on each side of the old Professor, the astonished commissionaire bringing up the rear. When we reached the violated case, Mortimer stopped and examined the breastplate. Already one of the stones of the lower row had had its setting turned back in the same manner as the others. My friend held it up and glanced furiously at his prisoner.

"How could you!" he cried. "How could you!"

"It is horrible—horrible!" said the Professor "I don't wonder at your feelings. Take me to your room."

"But this shall not be left exposed!" cried Mortimer. He picked the breastplate up and carried it tenderly in his hand, while I walked beside the professor, like a policeman with a malefactor. We passed into Mortimer's chambers, leaving the amazed old soldier to understand matters as best he could. The Professor sat down in Mortimer's armchair, and turned so ghastly a colour that for the instant, all our resentment was changed to concern. A stiff glass of brandy brought the life back to him once more.

"There, I am better now!" said he. "These last few days have been too much for me. I am convinced that I could not stand it any longer. It is a nightmare—a horrible nightmare—that I should be arrested as a burglar in what has been for so long my own museum. And yet I cannot blame you. You could not have done otherwise. My hope always was that I should get it all over before I was detected. This would have been my last night's work."

"How did you get in?" asked Mortimer.

"By taking a very great liberty with your private door. But the object justified it. The object justified everything. You will not be angry when you know everything—at least, you will not be angry with me. I had a key to your side door and also to the museum door. I did not give them up when I left. And so you see it was not difficult for me to let myself into the museum. I used to come in early before the crowd had cleared from the street. Then I hid myself in the mummy-case, and took refuge there whenever Simpson came round. I could always hear him coming. I used to leave in the same way as I came."

"You ran a risk."

"I had to."

"But why? What on earth was your object—*you* to do a thing like that!" Mortimer pointed reproachfully at the plate which lay before him on the table.

"I could devise no other means. I thought and thought, but there was no alternative except a hideous public scandal, and a private sorrow which would have clouded our lives. I acted for the best, incredible as it may seem to you, and I only ask your attention to enable me to prove it."

"I will hear what you have to say before I take any further steps," said Mortimer, grimly.

"I am determined to hold back nothing, and to take you both completely into my confidence. I will leave it to your own generosity how far you will use the facts with which I supply you."

"We have the essential facts already."

"And yet you understand nothing. Let me go back to what passed a few weeks ago, and I will make it all clear to you. Believe me that what I say is the absolute and exact truth.

"You have met the person who calls himself Captain Wilson. I say 'calls himself' because I have reason now to believe that it is not his correct name. It would take me too long if I were to describe all the means by which he obtained an introduction to me and ingratiated himself into my friendship and the affection of my daughter. He brought letters from foreign colleagues which compelled me to show him some attention. And then, by his own attainments, which are considerable, he succeeded in making himself a very welcome visitor at my rooms. When I learned that my daughter's affections had been gained by him, I may have thought it premature, but I certainly was not surprised, for he had a charm of manner and of conversation which would have made him conspicuous in any society.

"He was much interested in Oriental antiquities, and his knowledge of the subject justified his interest. Often when he spent the evening with us he would ask permission to go down into the museum and have an opportunity of privately inspecting the various specimens. You can imagine that I, as an enthusiast, was in sympathy with such a request, and that I felt no surprise at the constancy of his visits. After his actual engagement to Elise, there was hardly an evening which he did not pass with us, and an hour or two were generally devoted to the museum. He had the free run of the place, and when I have been away for the evening I had no objection to his doing what ever he wished here. This state of things was only terminated by the fact of my resignation of my official duties and my retirement to Norwood, where I hoped to have the leisure to write a considerable work which I had planned.

"It was immediately after this—within a week or so— that I first realized the true nature and character of the man whom I had so imprudently introduced into my family. The discovery came to me through letters from my friends abroad, which showed me that his introductions to me had been forgeries. Aghast at the revelation, I asked myself what motive this man could originally have had in practising this elaborate deception upon me. I was too poor a man for any fortune hunter to have marked me down. Why, then, had he come? I remembered that some of the most precious gems in Europe had been under my charge, and I remembered also the ingenious excuses by which this man had made himself familiar with the cases in which they were kept. He was a rascal who was planning some gigantic robbery. How could I, without striking my own daughter, who was infatuated about him, prevent him from carrying out any plan which he might have formed? My device was a clumsy one, and yet I could think of nothing more effective. If I had written a letter under my own name, you would naturally have turned to me for details which I did not wish to give. I resorted to an anonymous letter, begging you to be upon your guard.

"I may tell you that my change from Belmore Street to Norwood had not affected the visits of this man, who had, I believe, a real and overpowering affection for my daughter. As to her, I could not have believed that any woman could be so completely under the influence of a man as she was. His stronger nature seemed to entirely dominate her. I had not realized how far this was the case, or the extent of the confidence which existed between them, until that very evening when his true character for the first time was made clear to me. I had given orders that when he called he should be shown into my study instead of to the drawing-room. There I told him bluntly that I knew all about him, that I had taken steps to defeat his designs, and that neither I nor my daughter desired ever to see him again. I added that I thanked God that I had found him out before he had time to harm those precious objects which it had been the work of my lifetime to protect.

"He was certainly a man of iron nerve. He took my remarks without a sign either of surprise or of defiance, but listened gravely and attentively until I had finished. Then he walked across the room without a word and struck the bell.

"'Ask Miss Andreas to be so kind as to step this way,' said he to the servant.

"My daughter entered, and the man closed the door behind her. Then he took her hand in his.

"'Elise,' said he, 'your father has just discovered that I am a villain. He knows now what you knew before.'

"She stood in silence, listening.

"'He says that we are to part forever,' said he.

"She did not withdraw her hand.

"'Will you be true to me, or will you remove the last good influence which is ever likely to come into my life?'

"'John,' she cried, passionately, 'I will never abandon you! Never, never, not if the whole world were against you.'

"In vain I argued and pleaded with her. It was absolutely useless. Her whole life was bound up in this man before me. My daughter, gentlemen, is all that I have left to love, and it filled me with agony when I saw how pow-

erless I was to save her from her ruin. My helplessness
seemed to touch this man who was the cause of my trouble.

"'It may not be as bad as you think, sir,' said he, in his
quiet, inflexible way. 'I love Elise with a love which is
strong enough to rescue even one who has such a record
as I have. It was but yesterday that I promised her that
never again in my whole life would I do a thing of which
she should be ashamed. I have made up my mind to it, and
never yet did I make up my mind to a thing which I did not
do.'

"He spoke with an air which carried conviction with
it. As he concluded he put his hand into his pocket and he
drew out a small cardboard box.

"'I am about to give you a proof of my determination,'
said he. 'This, Elise, shall be the first fruits of your re-
deeming influence over me. You are right, sir, in thinking
that I had designs upon the jewels in your possession. Such
ventures have had a charm for me, which depended as much
upon the risk run as upon the value of the prize. Those
famous and antique stones of the Jewish priest were a challenge to my daring and my ingenuity. I determined to get
them.'

"'I guessed as much.'

"'There was only one thing that you did not guess.'

"'And what is that?"

"'That I got them. They are in this box.'

"He opened the box, and tilted out the contents upon
the corner of my desk. My hair rose and my flesh grew
cold as I looked. There were twelve magnificent square

stones engraved with mystical characters. There could be no doubt that they were the jewels of the urim and thummim.

"'Good God!' I cried. 'How have you escaped discovery?'

"By the substitution of twelve others, made especially to my order, in which the originals are so carefully imitated that I defy the eye to detect the difference.'

"'Then the present stones are false?' I cried.

"'They have been for some weeks.'

"We all stood in silence, my daughter white with emotion, but still holding this man by the hand.

"'You see what I am capable of, Elise,' said he.

"'I see that you are capable of repentance and restitution,' she answered.

"'Yes, thanks to your influence! I leave the stones in your hands, sir. Do what you like about it. But remember that whatever you do against me, is done against the future husband of your only daughter. You will hear from me soon again, Elise. It is the last time that I will ever cause pain to your tender heart,' and with these words he left both the room and the house.

"My position was a dreadful one. Here I was with these precious relics in my possession, and how could I return them without a scandal and an exposure? I knew the depth of my daughter's nature too well to suppose that I would ever be able to detach her from this man now that she had entirely given him her heart. I was not even sure how far it was right to detach her if she had such an ameliorating influence over him. How could I expose him without injuring her—and how far was I justified in exposing him when he had voluntarily put himself into my power? I thought and thought, until at last I formed a resolution which may seem to you to be a foolish one, and yet, if I had to do it again, I believe it would be the best course open to me.

"My idea was to return the stones without anyone being the wiser. With my keys I could get into the museum at any time, and I was confident that I could avoid Simpson, whose hours and methods were familiar to me. I determined to take no one into my confidence—not even my daughter—whom I told that I was about to visit my brother in Scotland. I wanted a free hand for a few nights, without inquiry as to my comings and goings. To this end I took a room in Harding Street that very night, with an intimation that I was a Pressman, and that I should keep very late hours.

"That night I made my way into the museum, and I replaced four of the stones. It was hard work, and took me all night. When Simpson came round I always heard his footsteps, and concealed myself in the mummy-case. I had some knowledge of gold work, but was far less skilful than the thief had been. He had replaced the setting so exactly that I defy any one to see the difference. My work was rude and clumsy. However, I hoped that the plate might not be carefully examined, or the roughness of the setting observed, until my task was done. Next night I replaced four more stones. And tonight I should have finished my task had it not been for the unfortunate circumstance which has caused me to reveal so much which I should have wished to keep concealed. I appeal to you, gentlemen, to your sense of honour and of compassion, whether what I have told you should go any farther or not. My own happiness, my daughter's future, the hopes of this man's regeneration, all depend upon your decision."

"Which is," said my friend, "that all is well that ends well, and that the whole matter ends here and at once. Tomorrow the loose settings shall be tightened by an expert goldsmith, and so passes the greatest danger to which, since the destruction of the Temple, the urim and thummim have been exposed. Here is my hand, Professor Andreas, and I can only hope that under such difficult circumstances I should have carried myself as unselfishly and as well."

Just one footnote to this narrative. Within a month Elise Andreas was married to a man whose name, had I the indiscretion to mention it, would appeal to my readers as one who is now widely and deservedly honoured. But if the truth were known, that honour is due not to him but to the gentle girl who plucked him back when he had gone so far down that dark road along which few return.

/ The Lost Special /

The confession of Herbert de Lernac, now lying under
sentence of death at Marseilles, has thrown a light upon
one of the most inexplicable crimes of the century—an
incident which is, I believe, absolutely unprecedented in
the criminal annals of any country. Although there is a re-
luctance to discuss the matter in official circles, and little
information has been given to the mess, there are still indications that the statement of this arch-criminal is corroborated by the facts, and that we have at last found a
solution for a most astounding business. As the matter is
eight years old, and as its importance was somewhat ob-
scured by a political crisis which was engaging the public
attention at the time, it may be as well to state the facts as
far as we have been able to ascertain them. They are col-
lated from the Liverpool papers of that date, from the proceedings at the inquest upon John Slater, the engine-driver,
and from the records of the London and West Coast Railway Company, which have been courteously put at my
disposal. Briefly, they are as follows.

On the 3rd of June, 1890, a gentleman, who gave his
name as Monsieur Louis Caratal, desired an interview with

Mr. James Bland, the superintendent of the London and West Coast Central Station in Liverpool.

He was a small man, middle-aged and dark, with a stoop which was so marked that it suggested some deformity of the spine. He was accompanied by a friend, a man of imposing physique, whose deferential manner and constant attention showed that his position was one of dependence. This friend or companion, whose name did not transpire, was certainly a foreigner, and probably, from his swarthy complexion, either a Spaniard or a South American. One peculiarity was observed in him. He carried in his left hand a small black leather dispatch-box, and it was noticed by a sharp-eyed clerk in the Central office that this box was fastened to his wrist by a strap. No importance was attached to the fact at the time, but subsequent events endowed it with some significance. Monsieur Caratal was shown up to Mr. Bland's office, while his companion remained outside.

Monsieur Caratal's business was quickly dispatched. He had arrived that afternoon from Central America. Affairs of the utmost importance demanded that he should be in Paris without the loss of an unnecessary hour. He had missed the London express. A special must be provided. Money was of no importance. Time was everything. If the company would speed him on his way, they might make their own terms.

Mr. Bland struck the electric bell, summoned Mr. Potter Hood, the track manager, and had the matter arranged in five minutes. The train would start in three-quarters of an hour. It would take that time to insure that the line should be clear. The powerful engine called Rochdale (No. 247 on the company's register) was attached to two carriages, with a guard's van behind. The first carriage was solely for the purpose of decreasing the inconvenience arising from the oscillation. The second was divided, as usual, into four compartments, a first-class, a first-class smoking, a second-class, and a second-class smoking. The first compartment, which was nearest to the engine, was the one allotted to the travellers. The other three were empty. The guard of the special train was James McPherson, who had been some years in the service of the company. The stoker, William Smith, was a new hand.

Monsieur Caratal, upon leaving the superintendent's office, rejoined his companion, and both of them manifested extreme impatience to be off. Having paid the money asked, which amounted to fifty pounds, five shillings, at the usual special rate of five shillings a mile, they demanded to be shown the carriage, and at once took their seats in it, although they were assured that the better part of an hour must elapse before the line could be cleared. In the meantime a singular coincidence had occurred in the office which Monsieur Caratal had just quitted.

A request for a special is not a very uncommon circumstance in a rich commercial centre, but that two should be required upon the same afternoon was most unusual. It so happened, however, that Mr. Bland had hardly dismissed the first traveller before a second entered with a similar request. This was a Mr. Horace Moore, a gentlemanly man of military appearance, who alleged that the sudden serious illness of his wife in London made it absolutely imperative that he should not lose an instant in starting upon the journey. His distress and anxiety were so evident that Mr. Bland did all that was possible to meet his wishes. A second special was out of the question, as the ordinary local service was already somewhat deranged by the first. There was the alternative, however, that Mr. Moore should share the expense of Monsieur Caratal's train, and should travel in the other empty first-class compartment, if Monsieur Caratal objected to having him in the one which he occupied. It was difficult to see any objection to such an arrangement, and yet Monsieur Caratal, upon the suggestion being made to him by Mr. Potter Hood, absolutely refused to consider it for an instant. The train was his, he said, and he would insist upon the exclusive use of it. All argument failed to overcome his ungracious objections, and finally the plan had to be abandoned. Mr. Horace Moore left the station in great distress, after learning that his only course was to take the ordinary slow train which leaves Liverpool at six o'clock. At 4.31 exactly by the station clock, the special train, containing the crippled Monsieur Caratal and his gigantic companion, steamed out of the Liverpool station. The line was at that time clear, and there should have been no stoppage before Manchester.

The trains of the London and West Coast Railway run over the lines of another company as far as this town, which should have been reached by the special rather before six o'clock. At a quarter after six considerable surprise and some consternation were caused amongst the officials at Liverpool by the receipt of a telegram from Manchester to say that it had not yet arrived. An inquiry directed to St. Helens, which is a third of the way between the two cities, elicited the following reply:—

"To James Bland, Superintendent, Central L. & W. C., Liverpool.—Special passed here at 4.52, well up to time.— Dowser, St. Helens."

This telegram was received at 6.40. At 6.50 a second message was received from Manchester:—

"No sign of special as advised by you."

And then ten minutes later a third, more bewildering:—

"Presume some mistake as to proposed running of special. Local train from St. Helens timed to follow it has just arrived and has seen nothing of it. Kindly wire advices.— Manchester."

The matter was assuming a most amazing aspect, although in some respects the last telegram was a relief to the authorities at Liverpool. If an accident had occurred to the special, it seemed hardly possible that the local train could have passed down the same line without observing it. And yet, what was the alternative? Where could the train be? Had it possibly been side-tracked for some reason in order to allow the slower train to go past? Such an explanation was possible if some small repair had to be effected. A telegram was dispatched to each of the stations between St. Helens and Manchester, and the superintendent and traffic manager waited in the utmost suspense at the instrument for the series of replies which would enable them to say for certain what had become of the missing train. The answers came back in the order of questions, which was the order of the stations beginning at the St. Helens end:—

"Special passed here five o'clock.—Collins Green."

"Special passed here six past five.—Earlestown."

"Special passed here 5.10.—Newton."

"Special passed here 5.20.—Kenyon Junction."

"No special train has passed here.—Barton Moss."

The two officials stared at each other in amazement.

"This is unique in my thirty years of experience," said Mr. Bland.

"Absolutely unprecedented and inexplicable, sir. The special has gone wrong between Kenyon Junction and Barton Moss."

"And yet there is no siding, so far as my memory serves me, between the two stations. The special must have run off the metals."

"But how could the four-fifty parliamentary pass over the same line without observing it?"

"There's no alternative, Mr. Hood. It *must* be so. Possibly the local train may have observed something which may throw some light upon the matter. We will wire to Manchester for more information, and to Kenyon Junction with instructions that the line be examined instantly as far as Barton Moss."

The answer from Manchester came within a few minutes.

"No news of missing special. Driver and guard of slow train positive no accident between Kenyon Junction and

Barton Moss. Line quite clear, and no sign of anything unusual.—Manchester."

"That driver and guard will have to go," said Mr. Bland, grimly. "There has been a wreck and they have missed it. The special has obviously run off the metals without disturbing the line—how it could have done so passes my comprehension—but so it must be, and we shall have a wire from Kenyon or Barton Moss presently to say that they have found her at the bottom of an embankment."

But Mr. Bland's prophecy was not destined to be fulfilled. Half an hour passed, and then there arrived the following message from the station-master of Kenyon Junction:—

"There are no traces of the missing special. It is quite certain that she passed here, and that she did not arrive at Barton Moss. We have detached engine from goods train, and I have myself ridden down the line, but all is clear, and there is no sign of any accident."

Mr. Bland tore his hair in his perplexity.

"This is rank lunacy, Hood!" he cried. "Does a train vanish into thin air in England in broad daylight? The thing is preposterous. An engine, a tender, two carriages, a van, five human beings—and all lost on a straight line of railway! Unless we get something positive within the next hour I'll take Inspector Collins, and go down myself."

And then at last something positive did occur. It took the shape of another telegram from Kenyon Junction.

"Regret to report that the dead body of John Slater, driver of the special train, has just been found among the gorse bushes at a point two and a quarter miles from the Junction. Had fallen from his engine, pitched down the embankment, and rolled among bushes. Injuries to his head, from the fall, appear to be cause of death. Ground has now been carefully examined, and there is no trace of the missing train."

The country was, as has already been stated, in the throes of a political crisis, and the attention of the public was further distracted by the important and sensational developments in Paris, where a huge scandal threatened to destroy the Government and to wreck the reputations of many of the leading men in France. The papers were full of these events, and the singular disappearance of the special train attracted less attention than would have been the case in more peaceful times. The grotesque nature of the event helped to detract from its importance, for the papers were disinclined to believe the facts as reported to them. More than one of the London journals treated the matter as an ingenious hoax, until the coroners inquest upon the unfortunate driver (an inquest which elicited nothing of importance) convinced them of the tragedy of the incident.

Mr. Bland, accompanied by Inspector Collins, the senior detective officer in the service of the company, went down to Kenyon Junction the same evening, and their research lasted throughout the following day, but was attended with purely negative results. Not only was no trace found of the missing train, but no conjecture could be put forward which could possibly explain the facts. At the same time, Inspector Collins's official report (which lies before me as I write) served to show that the possibilities were more numerous than might have been expected.

"In the stretch of railway between these two points," said he, "the country is dotted with ironworks and collieries. Of these, some are being worked and some have been abandoned. There are no fewer than twelve which have small gauge lines which run trolly cars down to the main line. These can, of course, be disregarded. Besides these, however, there are seven which have or have had, proper lines running down and connecting with points to the main line, so as to convey their produce from the mouth of the mine to the great centres of distribution. In every case these lines are only a few miles in length. Out of the seven, four belong to collieries which are worked out, or at least to shafts which are no longer used. These are the Redgauntlet, Hero, Slough of Despond, and Heartsease mines, the latter having ten years ago been one of the principal mines in Lancashire. These four side lines may be eliminated from our inquiry, for, to prevent possible accidents, the rails nearest to the main line have been taken up, and there is no longer any connection. There remain three other side lines leading—

(a) To the Carnstock Iron Works;

(b) To the Big Ben Colliery;

(c) To the Perseverance Colliery.

"Of these the Big Ben line is not more than a quarter of a mile long, and ends at a dead wall of coal waiting removal from the mouth of the mine. Nothing had been seen or heard there of any special. The Carnstock Iron Works line was blocked all day upon the 3rd of June by sixteen truckloads of hematite. It is a single line, and nothing could have passed. As to the Perseverance line, it is a large double line, which does a considerable traffic, for the output of the mine is very large. On the 3rd of June this traffic proceeded as usual; hundreds of men, including a gang of railway platelayers, were working along the two miles and a quarter which constitute the total length of the line, and it is inconceivable that an unexpected train could have come down there without attracting universal attention. It may be remarked in conclusion that this branch line is nearer to St. Helens than the point at which the engine-driver was discovered, so that we have every reason to believe that the train was past that point before misfortune overtook her.

"As to John Slater, there is no clue to be gathered from his appearance or injuries. We can only say that, so far as we can see, he met his end by falling off his engine, though why he fell, or what became of the engine after his fall, is a question upon which I do not feel qualified to offer an opinion." In conclusion, the inspector offered his resignation to the Board, being much nettled by an accusation of incompetence in the London papers.

A month elapsed, during which both the police and the company prosecuted their inquiries without the slightest success. A reward was offered and a pardon promised in case of crime, but they were both unclaimed. Every day the public opened their papers with the conviction that so grotesque a mystery would at last be solved, but week after week passed by, and a solution remained as far off as ever. In broad daylight, upon a June afternoon in the most thickly inhabited portion of England, a train with its occupants had disappeared as completely as if some master of subtle chemistry had volatilized it into gas. Indeed, among the various conjectures which were put forward in the public Press there were some which seriously asserted that supernatural, or, at least, preternatural, agencies had been at work, and that the deformed Monsieur Caratal was probably a person who was better known under a less polite name. Others fixed upon his swarthy companion as being the author of the mischief, but what it was exactly which he had done could never be clearly formulated in words.

Amongst the many suggestions put forward by various newspapers or private individuals, there were one or two which were feasible enough to attract the attention of the public. One which appeared in the *Times,* over the signature of an amateur reasoner of some celebrity at that date, attempted to deal with the matter in a critical and semi-scientific manner. An extract must suffice, although the curious can see the whole letter in the issue of the 3rd of July.

"It is one of the elementary principles of practical reasoning," he remarked, "that when the impossible had been eliminated the residuum, *however improbable,* must contain the truth. It is certain that the train left Kenyon Junction. It is certain that it did not reach Barton Moss. It is in the highest degree unlikely, but still possible, that it may have taken one of the seven available side lines. It is obviously impossible for a train to run where there are no rails, and, therefore, we may reduce our improbables to the three open lines, namely, the Carnstock Iron Works, the Big Ben, and the Perseverance. Is there a secret society of colliers, an English *camorra,* which is capable of destroying both train and passengers? It is improbable, but it is not impossible. I confess that I am unable to suggest any other solution. I should certainly advise the company to direct all their energies towards the observation of those three lines, and of the workmen at the end of them. A careful supervision of the pawnbrokers' shops of the district might possibly bring some suggestive facts to light."

The suggestion coming from a recognized authority upon such matters created considerable interest, and a fierce opposition from those who considered such a statement to be a preposterous libel upon an honest and deserving set of men. The only answer to this criticism was a challenge to the objectors to lay any more feasible explanation before the public. In reply to this, two others were forthcoming (*Times*, July 7th and 9th). The first suggested that the train might have run off the metals and be lying submerged in the Lancashire and Staffordshire Canal, which runs parallel to the railway for some hundreds of yards. This suggestion was thrown out of court by the published depth of the canal, which was entirely insufficient to conceal so large an object. The second correspondent wrote calling attention to the bag which appeared to be the sole luggage which the travellers had brought with them, and suggest-

ing that some novel explosive of immense and pulveriz-
ing power might have been concealed in it. The obvious
absurdity, however, of supposing that the whole train might
be blown to dust while the metals remained uninjured re-
duced any such explanation to a farce. The investigation
had drifted into this hopeless position when a new and
most unexpected incident occurred.

This was nothing less than the receipt by Mrs.
McPherson of a letter from her husband, James McPherson,
who had been the guard of the missing train. The letter,
which was dated July 5th, 1890, was posted from New
York, and came to hand upon July 14th. Some doubts were
expressed as to its genuine character, but Mrs. McPherson
was positive as to the writing, and the fact that it contained
a remittance of a hundred dollars in five-dollar notes was
enough in itself to discount the idea of a hoax. No address
was given in the letter, which ran in this way:—

"My Dear Wife,—
"I have been thinking a great deal, and I find it very
hard to give you up. The same with Lizzie. I try to
fight against it, but it will always come back to me. I
send you some money which will change into twenty
English pounds. This should be enough to bring both
Lizzie and you across the Atlantic, and you will find
the Hamburg boats which stop at Southampton very
good boats, and cheaper than Liverpool. If you could
come here and stop at the Johnston House I would
try and send you word how to meet, but things are

very difficult with me at present, and I am not very happy, finding it hard to give you both up. So no more at present, from your loving husband,

"James McPherson."

For a time it was confidently anticipated that this letter would lead to the clearing up of the whole matter, the more so as it was ascertained that a passenger who bore a close resemblance to the missing guard had travelled from Southampton under the name of Summers in the Hamburg and New York liner *Vistula,* which started upon the 7th of June. Mrs. McPherson and her sister Lizzie Dolton went across to New York as directed, and stayed for three weeks at the Johnston House, without hearing anything from the missing man. It is probable that some injudicious comments in the Press may have warned him that the police were using them as a bait. However this may be, it is certain that he neither wrote nor came, and the women were eventually compelled to return to Liverpool.

And so the matter stood, and has continued to stand up to the present year of 1898. Incredible as it may seem, nothing has transpired during these eight years which has shed the least light upon the extraordinary disappearance of the special train which contained Monsieur Caratal and his companion. Careful inquiries into the antecedents of the two travellers have only established the fact that Monsieur Caratal was well known as a financier and political agent in Central America, and that during his voyage to Europe he had betrayed extraordinary anxiety to reach

Paris. His companion, whose name was entered upon the passenger lists as Eduardo Gomez, was a man whose record was a violent one, and whose reputation was that of a bravo and a bully. There was evidence to show, however, that he was honestly devoted to the interests of Monsieur Caratal, and that the latter, being a man of puny physique, employed the other as a guard and protector. It may be added that no information came from Paris as to what the objects of Monsieur Caratal's hurried journey may have been. This comprises all the facts of the case up to the publication in the Marseilles papers of the recent confession of Herbert de Lernac, now under sentence of death for the murder of a merchant named Bonvalot. This statement may be literally translated as follows:—

"It is not out of mere pride or boasting that I give this information, for, if that were my object, I could tell a dozen actions of mine which are quite as splendid; but I do it in order that certain gentlemen in Paris may understand that I, who am able here to tell about the fate of Monsieur Caratal, can also tell in whose interest and at whose request the deed was done, unless the reprieve which I am awaiting comes to me very quickly. Take warning, messieurs, before it is too late! You know Herbert de Lernac, and you are aware that his deeds are as ready as his words. Hasten then, or you are lost!

"At present I shall mention no names—if you only heard the names, what would you not think!—but I shall merely tell you how cleverly I did it. I was true to my employers then, and no doubt they will be true to me now.

I hope so, and until I am convinced that they have betrayed me, these names, which would convulse Europe, shall not be divulged. But on that day. . . well, I say no more!

"In a word, then, there was a famous trial in Paris, in the year 1890, in connection with a monstrous scandal in politics and finance. How monstrous that scandal was can never be known save by such confidential agents as myself. The honour and careers of many of the chief men in France were at stake. You have seen a group of nine-pins standing, all so rigid, and prim, and unbending. Then there comes the ball from far away and pop, pop, pop—there are your nine-pins on the floor. Well, imagine some of the greatest men in France as these nine-pins, and then this Monsieur Caratal was the ball which could be seen coming from far away. If he arrived, then it was pop, pop, pop for all of them. It was determined that he should not arrive.

"I do not accuse them all of being conscious of what was to happen. There were, as I have said, great financial as well as political interests at stake, and a syndicate was formed to manage the business. Some subscribed to the syndicate who hardly understood what were its objects. But others understood very well, and they can rely upon it that I have not forgotten their names. They had ample warning that Monsieur Caratal was coming long before he left South America, and they knew that the evidence which he held would certainly mean ruin to all of them. The syndicate had the command of an unlimited amount of money—absolutely unlimited, you understand. They looked round for an agent who was capable of wielding this gigantic power. The man chosen must be inventive, resolute, adaptive—a man in a million. They chose Herbert de Lernac, and I admit that they were right.

"My duties were to choose my subordinates, to use freely the power which money gives, and to make certain that Monsieur Caratal should never arrive in Paris. With characteristic energy I set about my commission within an hour of receiving my instructions, and the steps which I took were the very best for the purpose which could possibly be devised.

"A man whom I could trust was dispatched instantly to South America to travel home with Monsieur Caratal. Had he arrived in time the ship would never have reached Liverpool; but, alas! it had already started before my agent could reach it. I fitted out a small armed brig to intercept it, but again I was unfortunate. Like all great organizers I was, however, prepared for failure, and had a series of alternatives prepared, one or the other of which must succeed. You must not underrate the difficulties of my undertaking, or imagine that a mere commonplace assassination would meet the case. We must destroy not only Monsieur Caratal, but Monsieur Caratal's documents, and Monsieur Caratal's companions also, if we had reason to believe that he had communicated his secrets to them. And you must remember that they were on the alert, and keenly suspicious of any such attempt. It was a task which was in every way worthy of me, for I am always most masterful where another would be appalled.

"I was all ready for Monsieur Caratal's reception in Liverpool, and I was the more eager because I had reason to believe that he had made arrangements by which he would have a considerable guard from the moment that he arrived in London. Anything which was to be done must be done between the moment of his setting foot upon the Liverpool quay and that of his arrival at the London and West Coast terminus in London. We prepared six plans, each more elaborate than the last; which plan would be used would depend upon his own movements. Do what he would, we were ready for him. If he had stayed in Liverpool, we were ready. If he took an ordinary train, an express, or a special, all was ready. Everything had been foreseen and provided for.

"You may imagine that I could not do all this myself. What could I know of the English railway lines? But money can procure willing agents all the world over, and I soon had one of the acutest brains in England to assist me. I will mention no names, but it would be unjust to claim all the credit for myself. My English ally was worthy of such an alliance. He knew the London and West Coast line thoroughly, and he had the command of a band of workers who were trustworthy and intelligent. The idea was his, and my own judgment was only required in the details. We bought over several officials, amongst whom the most important was James McPherson, whom we had ascertained to be the guard most likely to be employed upon a special train. Smith, the stoker, was also in our employ. John Slater, the engine-driver, had been approached, but had been found to be obstinate and dangerous, so we desisted. We had no certainty that Monsieur Caratal would take a special, but we thought it very probable, for it was of the utmost importance to him that he should reach Paris without delay. It was for this contingency, therefore, that we made special preparation—preparations which were complete down to the last detail long before his steamer had sighted the shores of England. You will be amused to learn that there was one of my agents in the pilot-boat which brought that steamer to its moorings.

"The moment that Caratal arrived in Liverpool we knew that he suspected danger and was on his guard. He had brought with him as an escort a dangerous fellow named Gomez, a man who carried weapons, and was prepared to use them. This fellow carried Caratal's confidential papers for him, and was ready to protect either them or his master. The probability was that Caratal had taken him into his counsels, and that to remove Caratal without removing Gomez would be a mere waste of energy. It was necessary that they should be involved in a common fate, and our plans to that end were much facilitated by their request for a special train. On that special train you will understand that two out of the three servants of the company were really in our employ, at a price which would make them independent for a lifetime. I do not go so far as to say that the English are more honest than any other nation, but I have found them more expensive to buy.

"I have already spoken of my English agent—who is a man with a considerable future before him, unless some complaint of the throat carries him off before his time. He had charge of all arrangements at Liverpool, whilst I was stationed at the inn at Kenyon, where I awaited a cipher signal to act. When the special was arranged for, my agent instantly telegraphed to me and warned me how soon I should have everything ready. He himself, under the name of Horace Moore, applied immediately for a special also, in the hope that he would be sent down with Monsieur Caratal, which might under certain circumstances have been helpful to us. If, for example, our great *coup* had failed, it would then have become the duty of my agent to have shot them both and destroyed their papers. Caratal was on his guard, however, and refused to admit any other traveller. My agent then left the station, returned by another entrance, entered the guard's van on the side farthest from the platform, and travelled down with McPherson the guard.

"In the meantime you will be interested to know what my movements were. Everything had been prepared for days before, and only the finishing touches were needed. The side line which we had chosen had once joined the main line, but it had been disconnected. We had only to replace a few rails to connect it once more. These rails had been laid down as far as could be done without danger of attracting attention, and now it was merely a case of completing a juncture with the line, and arranging the points as they had been before. The sleepers had never been removed, and the rails, fish-plates, and rivets were all ready, for we had taken them from a siding on the abandoned portion of the line. With my small but competent band of workers, we had everything ready long before the special arrived. When it did arrive, it ran off upon the small side line so easily that the jolting of the points appears to have been entirely unnoticed by the two travellers.

"Our plan had been that Smith the stoker should chloroform John Slater the driver, so that he should vanish with the others. In this respect, and in this respect only, our plans miscarried—I except the criminal folly of McPherson in writing home to his wife. Our stoker did his business so clumsily that Slater in his struggles fell off the engine, and though fortune was with us so far that he broke his neck in the fall, still he remained as a blot upon that which would otherwise have been one of those complete masterpieces which are only to be contemplated in silent admiration. The criminal expert will find in John Slater the one flaw in all our admirable combinations. A man who has had as many triumphs as I, can afford to be frank, and I therefore lay my finger upon John Slater, and I proclaim him to be a flaw.

"But now I have got our special train upon the small line two kilomètres, or rather more than one mile, in length, which leads, or rather used to lead, to the abandoned Heartsease mine, once one of the largest coal mines in England. You will ask how it is that no one saw the train upon this unused line. I answer that along its entire length it runs through a deep cutting, and that, unless someone had been on the edge of that cutting, he could not have seen it. There *was* someone on the edge of that cutting. I was there. And now I will tell you what I saw.

"My assistant had remained at the points in order that he might superintend the switching off of the train. He had four armed men with him, so that if the train ran off the line—we thought it probable, because the points were very rusty—we might still have resources to fall back upon. Having once seen it safely on the side line, he handed over the responsibility to me. I was waiting at a point which overlooks the mouth of the mine, and I was also armed, as were my two companions. Come what might, you see, I was always ready.

"The moment that the train was fairly on the side line, Smith, the stoker, slowed down the engine, and then, having turned it on to the fullest speed again, he and McPherson, with my English lieutenant, sprang off before it was too late. It may be that it was this slowing-down which first attracted the attention of the travellers, but the train was running at full speed again before their heads appeared at the open window. It makes me smile to think how bewildered they must have been. Picture to yourself your own feelings if, on looking out of your luxurious carriage, you suddenly perceived that the lines upon which you ran were rusted and corroded, red and yellow with disuse and decay! What a catch must have come in their breath as in a second it flashed upon them that it was not Manchester but Death which was waiting for them at the end of that sinister line. But the train was running with frantic speed, rolling and rocking over the rotten line, while the wheels made a frightful screaming sound upon the rusted surface. I was close to them, and could see their faces. Caratal was praying, I think—there was something like a rosary dangling out of his hand. The other roared like a bull who smells the blood of the slaughter-house. He saw us standing on the bank, and he beckoned to us like a madman. Then he tore at his wrist and threw his dispatch-box out of the window in our direction. Of course, his meaning was obvious. Here was the evidence, and they would promise to be silent if their lives were spared. It would have been very agreeable if we could have done so, but business is business. Besides, the train was now as much beyond our control as theirs.

"He ceased howling when the train rattled round the curve and they saw the black mouth of the mine yawning before them. We had removed the boards which had covered it, and we had cleared the square entrance. The rails had formerly run very close to the shaft for the convenience of loading the coal, and we had only to add two or three lengths of rail in order to lead to the very brink of the shaft. In fact, as the lengths would not quite fit, our line projected about three feet over the edge. We saw the two heads at the window: Caratal below, Gomez above; but they had both been struck silent by what they saw. And yet they could not withdraw their heads. The sight seemed to have paralyzed them.

"I had wondered how the train running at a great speed would take the pit into which I had guided it, and I was much interested in watching it. One of my colleagues thought that it would actually jump it, and indeed it was not very far from doing so. Fortunately, however, it fell

short, and the buffers of the engine struck the other lip of
the shaft with a tremendous crash The funnel flew off into
the air. The tender, carriages, and van were all smashed up
into one jumble, which, with the remains of the engine,
choked for a minute or so the mouth of the pit. Then something gave way in the middle, and the whole mass of green
iron, smoking coals, brass fittings, wheels, woodwork, and
cushions all crumbled together and crashed down into the
mine. We heard the rattle, rattle, rattle, as the *débris* struck
against the walls, and then quite a long time afterwards
there came a deep roar as the remains of the train struck
the bottom. The boiler may have burst, for a sharp crash
came after the roar, and then a dense cloud of steam and
smoke swirled up out of the black depths, falling in a spray
as thick as rain all round us. Then the vapour shredded off
into thin wisps, which floated away in the summer sun-
shine, and all was quiet again in the Heartsease mine.

"And now, having carried out our plans so success-
fully, it only remained to leave no trace behind us. Our
little band of workers at the other end had already ripped
up the rails and disconnected the side line, replacing everything as it had been before. We were equally busy at
the mine. The funnel and other fragments were thrown in,
the shaft was planked over as it used to be, and the lines
which led to it were torn up and taken away. Then, without flurry, but without delay, we all made our way out of
the country, most of us to Paris, my English colleague to
Manchester, and McPherson to Southampton, whence he
emigrated to America. Let the English papers of that date

tell how thoroughly we had done our work, and how completely we had thrown the cleverest of their detectives off our track.

"You will remember that Gomez threw his bag of papers out of the window, and I need not say that I secured that bag and brought them to my employers. It may interest my employers now, however, to learn that out of that bag I took one or two little papers as a souvenir of the occasion. I have no wish to publish these papers; but, still, it is every man for himself in this world, and what else can I do if my friends will not come to my aid when I want them? Messieurs, you may believe that Herbert de Lernac is quite as formidable when he is against you as when he is with you, and that he is not a man to go to the guillotine until he has seen that every one of you is *en route* for New Caledonia. For your own sake, if not for mine, make haste, Monsieur de ———— and General ————, and Baron ———— (you can fill up the blanks for yourselves as you read this). I promise you that in the next edition there will be no blanks to fill.

"P.S.—As I look over my statement, there is only one omission which I can see. It concerns the unfortunate man McPherson, who was foolish enough to write to his wife and to make an appointment with her in New York. It can be imagined that when interests like ours were at stake, we could not leave them to the chance of whether a man in that class of life would or would not give away his secrets to a woman. Having once broken his oath by writing to his wife, we could not trust him any more. We took steps there-

fore to insure that he should not see his wife. I have sometimes thought that it would be a kindness to write to her
and to assure her that there is no impediment to her marry-
ing again."

/ The Club-Footed Grocer /

My uncle, Mr. Stephen Maple, had been at the same time the most successful and the least respectable of our family, so that we hardly knew whether to take credit for his wealth or to feel ashamed of his position. He had, as a matter of fact, established a large grocery in Stepney which did a curious mixed business, not always, as we had heard, of a very savoury character, with the riverside and seafaring people. He was ship's chandler, provision merchant, and, if rumour spoke truly, some other things as well. Such a trade, however lucrative, had its drawbacks, as was evident when, after twenty years of prosperity, he was savagely assaulted in the Stepney Highway by one of his customers and left for dead, with three smashed ribs and a broken leg, which mended so badly that it remained forever three inches shorter than the other. This incident seemed, not unnaturally, to disgust him with his surroundings, for after the trial, in which his assailant was condemned to fifteen years' penal servitude, he retired from his business and settled in a lonely part of the North of England, whence, until that morning, we had never once heard of him—not even at the death of my father, who was his only brother. My mother read his letter aloud to me: "If your son is with you, Ellen, and if he is as stout a lad as he promised for when last I heard from you, then send him up to me by the first train after this comes to hand. He will find that to serve me will pay him better than the engineering, and if I pass away (though, thank God, there is no reason to complain as to my health) you will see that I have not forgotten my brother's son. Congleton is the station, and then a drive of four miles to Greta House, where I am now living. I will send a trap to meet the seven o'clock train, for it is the only one which stops here. Mind that you send him, Ellen, for I have very strong reasons for wishing him to be with me. Let bygones be bygones if there has been anything between us in the past. If you should fail me now, you will live to regret it."

We were seated at either side of the breakfast table, looking blankly at each other and wondering what this might mean, when there came a ring at the bell, and the maid walked in with a telegram. It was from Uncle Stephen.

"On no account let John get out at Congleton," said the message. "He will find trap waiting seven o'clock evening train Stedding Bridge, one station further down line. Let him drive not to me, but Garth Farm House—six miles. There will receive instructions. Do not fail; only you to look to."

"That is true enough," said my mother. "As far as I know, your uncle has not a friend in the world, nor has he ever deserved one. He has always been a hard man in his dealings, and he held back his money from your father at a time when a few pounds would have saved him from ruin. Why should I send my only son to serve him now?" But my own inclinations were all for the adventure.

"If I have him for a friend, he can help me in my profession," I argued, taking my mother upon her weakest side.

"I have never known him to help any one yet," said she, bitterly. "And why all this mystery about getting out at a distant station and driving to the wrong address? He has got himself into some trouble and he wishes us to get him out of it. When he has used us he will throw us aside as he has done before. Your father might have been living now if he had only helped him."

But at last my arguments prevailed, for, as I pointed out, we had much to gain and little to lose, and why should we, the poorest members of a family, go out of our way to offend the rich one? My bag was packed and my cab at the door, when there came a second telegram.

"Good shooting. Let John bring gun. Remember Stedding Bridge, not Congleton." And so, with a gun case added to my luggage and some surprise at my uncle's insistence, I started off upon my adventure.

The journey lies over the main Northern Railway as far as the station of Carnfield, where one changes for the little branch line which winds over the fells. In all England there is no harsher or more impressive scenery. For two hours, I passed through desolate rolling plains, rising at places into low, stone-littered hills, with long, straight outcrops of jagged rock showing upon their surface. Here and there little grey-roofed, grey-walled cottages huddled into villages, but for many miles at a time no house was visible, nor any sign of life save the scattered sheep which wandered over the mountainsides. It was a depressing country, and my heart grew heavier and heavier as I neared my journey's end, until at last the train pulled up at the little village of Stedding Bridge, where my uncle had told me to alight. A single ramshackle trap, with a country lout to drive it, was waiting at the station. "Is this Mr. Stephen Maple's?" I asked.

The fellow looked at me with eyes which were full of suspicion. "What is your name?" he asked, speaking a dialect which I will not attempt to reproduce.

"John Maple."

"Anything to prove it?"

I half-raised my hand, for my temper is none of the best, and then I reflected that the fellow was probably only carrying out the directions of my uncle. For answer I pointed to my name printed upon my gun-case.

"Yes, yes, that is right. It's John Maple, sure enough!" said he, slowly spelling it out. "Get in, maister, for we have a bit of a drive before us."

The road, white and shining, like all the roads in that limestone country, ran in long sweeps over the fells, with low walls of loose stone upon either side of it. The huge moors, mottled with sheep and with boulders, rolled away in gradually ascending curves to the misty skyline. In one place a fall of the land gave a glimpse of a grey angle of distant sea. Bleak and sad and stern were all my surroundings, and I felt, under their influence, that this curious mission of mine was a more serious thing than it had appeared when viewed from London. This sudden call for help from an uncle whom I had never seen, and of whom I had heard little that was good, the urgency of it, his reference to my physical powers, the excuse by which he had ensured that I should bring a weapon, all hung together and pointed to some vague but sinister meaning. Things which appeared to be impossible in Kensington became very probable upon these wild and isolated hillsides. At last, oppressed with my own dark thoughts, I turned to my companion with the intention of asking some questions about my uncle, but the expression upon his face drove the idea from my head.

He was not looking at his old, unclipped chestnut horse, nor at the road along which he was driving, but his face was turned in my direction, and he was staring past me with an expression of curiosity and, as I thought, of apprehension. He raised the whip to lash the horse, and then dropped it again, as if convinced that it was useless. At the same time, following the direction of his gaze, I saw what it was which had excited him.

A man was running across the moor. He ran clumsily, stumbling and slipping among the stones; but the road curved, and it was easy for him to cut us off. As we came up to the spot for which he had been making, he scrambled over the stone wall and stood waiting, with the evening sun shining on his brown, clean-shaven face. He was a burly fellow, and in bad condition, for he stood with his hand on his ribs, panting and blowing after his short run. As we drove up I saw the glint of earrings in his ears.

"Say, mate, where are you bound for?" he asked, in a rough but good-humoured fashion.

"Farmer Purcell's, at the Garth Farm," said the driver.

"Sorry to stop you," cried the other, standing aside; "I thought as I would hail you as you passed, for if so be as you had been going my way I should have made bold to ask you for a passage."

His excuse was an absurd one, since it was evident that our little trap was as full as it could be, but my driver did not seem disposed to argue. He drove on without a word, and, looking back, I could see the stranger sitting by the roadside and cramming tobacco into his pipe.

"A sailor," said I.

"Yes, maister. We're not more than a few miles from Morecambe Bay," the driver remarked.

"You seemed frightened of him," I observed.

"Did I?" said he, drily; and then, after a long pause, "Maybe I was." As to his reasons for fear, I could get nothing from him, and though I asked him many questions, he was so stupid, or else so clever, that I could learn nothing from his replies. I observed, however, that from time to time he swept the moors with a troubled eye, but their huge brown expanse was unbroken by any moving figure. At last in a sort of cleft in the hills in front of us I saw a long, low-lying farm building, the centre of all those scattered flocks.

"Garth Farm," said my driver. "There is Farmer Purcell himself," he added, as a man strolled out of the porch and stood waiting for our arrival. He advanced and descended from the trap, a hard, weather-worn fellow with light blue eyes, and hair and beard like sun-bleached grass. In his expression I read the same surly ill-will which I had already observed in my driver. Their malevolence could not be directed towards a complete stranger like myself, and so I began to suspect that my uncle was no more popular on the north-country fells than he had been in Stepney Highway.

"You're to stay here until nightfall. That's Mr. Stephen Maple's wish," said he, curtly. "You can have some tea and bacon if you like. It's the best we can give you."

I was very hungry, and accepted the hospitality in spite of the churlish tone in which it was offered. The farmer's wife and his two daughters came into the sitting-room during the meal, and I was aware of a certain curiosity with which they regarded me. It may have been that a young man was a rarity in this wilderness, or it may be that my attempts at conversation won their goodwill, but they all three showed a kindliness in their manner. It was getting dark, so I remarked that it was time for me to be pushing on to Greta House.

"You've made up your mind to go, then?" said the older woman.

"Certainly. I have come all the way from London."

"There's no one hindering you from going back there."

"But I have come to see Mr. Maple, my uncle."

"Oh, well, no one can stop you if you want to go on," said the woman, and became silent as her husband entered the room.

With every fresh incident I felt that I was moving in an atmosphere of mystery and peril, and yet it was all so intangible and so vague that I could not guess where my danger lay. I should have asked the farmer's wife point-blank, but her surly husband seemed to divine the sympathy which she felt for me, and never again left us together. "It's time you were going, mister," said he at last, as his wife lit the lamp upon the table.

"Is the trap ready?"

"You'll need no trap. You'll walk," said he.

"How shall I know the way?"

"William will go with you."

William was the youth who had driven me up from the station. He was waiting at the door, and he shouldered my gun-case and bag. I stayed behind to thank the farmer for his hospitality, but he would have none of it. "I ask no thanks from Mr. Stephen Maple nor any friend of his," said he, bluntly. "I am paid for what I do. If I was not paid I would not do it. Go your way, young man, and say no more." He turned rudely on his heel and re-entered his house, slamming the door behind him.

It was quite dark outside, with heavy black clouds drifting slowly across the sky. Once clear of the farm inclosure and out on the moor, I should have been hopelessly lost if it had not been for my guide, who walked in front of me along narrow sheep-tracks which were quite invisible to me. Every now and then, without seeing anything, we heard the clumsy scuffling of the creatures in the darkness. At first my guide walked swiftly and carelessly, but gradually his pace slowed down, until at last he was going very slowly and stealthily, like one who walks light-footed amid imminent menace. This vague, inexplicable sense of danger in the midst of the loneliness of that vast moor was more daunting than any evident peril could be, and I had begun to press him as to what it was that he feared, when suddenly he stopped and dragged me down among some gorse bushes which lined the path. His tug at my coat was so strenuous and imperative that I realized that the danger was a pressing one, and in an instant I was squatting down beside him as still as the bushes which shadowed us, It was so dark there that I could not even see the lad beside me.

It was a warm night, and a hot wind puffed in our faces. Suddenly in this wind there came something homely and familiar—the smell of burning tobacco. And then a face, illuminated by the glowing bowl of a pipe, came floating towards us. The man was all in shadow, but just that one dim halo of light with the face which filled it, brighter below and shading away into darkness above, stood out against the universal blackness. A thin, hungry face, thickly freckled with yellow over the cheek bones, blue, watery eyes, an ill-nourished, light-coloured moustache, a peaked yachting cap—that was all that I saw. He passed us, looking vacantly in front of him, and we heard the steps dying away along the path.

"Who was it?" I asked, as we rose to our feet.

"I don't know."

The fellow's continual profession of ignorance made me angry.

"Why should you hide yourself, then?" I asked, sharply.

"Because Maister Maple told me. He said that I were to meet no one. If I met any one I should get no pay."

"You met that sailor on the road?"

"Yes, and I think he was one of them."

"One of whom?"

"One of the folk that have come on the fells. They are watchin' Greta House, and Maister Maple is afeard of them. That's why he wanted us to keep clear of them, and that's why I've been a-trying to dodge 'em."

Here was something definite at last. Some body of men were threatening my uncle. The sailor was one of them. The man with the peaked cap—probably a sailor also—was another. I bethought me of Stepney Highway and of the murderous assault made upon my uncle there. Things were fitting themselves into a connected shape in my mind when a light twinkled over the fell, and my guide informed me that it was Greta House. The place lay in a dip among the moors, so that one was very near it before one saw it. A short walk brought us up to the door.

I could see little of the building save that the lamp which shone through a small latticed window showed me dimly that it was both long and lofty. The low door under an overhanging lintel was loosely fitted, and light was bursting out on each side of it. The inmates of this lonely house appeared to be keenly on their guard, for they had heard our footsteps, and we were challenged before we reached the door.

"Who is there?" cried a deep-booming voice, and urgently, "Who is it, I say?"

"It's me, Maister Maple. I have brought the gentleman."

There was a sharp click, and a small wooden shutter flew open in the door. The gleam of a lantern shone upon us for a few seconds. Then the shutter closed again; with a great rasping of locks and clattering of bars, the door was opened, and I saw my uncle standing framed in that vivid yellow square cut out of the darkness.

He was a small, thick man, with a great rounded, bald head and one thin border of gingery curls. It was a fine head, the head of a thinker, but his large white face was heavy and commonplace, with a broad, loose-lipped mouth and two hanging dewlaps on either side of it. His eyes were small and restless, and his light-coloured lashes were continually moving. My mother had said once that they reminded her of the legs of a woodlouse, and I saw at the first glance what she meant. I heard also that in Stepney he had learned the language of his customers, and I blushed for our kinship as I listened to his villainous accent. "So, nephew," said he, holding out his hand. "Come in, come in, man, quick, and don't leave the door open. Your mother said you were grown a big lad, and, my word, she 'as a right to say so. 'Ere's a 'alf-crown for you, William, and you can go back again. Put the thing down. 'Ere, Enoch, take Mr. John's things, and see that 'is supper is on the table."

As my uncle, after fastening the door, turned to show me into the sitting-room, I became aware of his most striking peculiarity. The injuries which he had received some years ago had, as I have already remarked, left one leg several inches shorter than the other. To atone for this, he wore one of those enormous wooden soles to his boots which are prescribed by surgeons in such cases. He walked without a limp, but his tread on the stone flooring made a curious clack-click, clack-click, as the wood and the leather alternated. Whenever he moved it was to the rhythm of this singular castanet.

The great kitchen, with its huge fireplace and carved settle corners, showed that this dwelling was an oldtime farmhouse. On one side of the room a line of boxes stood all corded and packed. The furniture was scant and plain, but on a trestle-table in the centre some supper, cold meat, bread, and a jug of beer was laid for me. An elderly man-servant, as manifest a Cockney as his master, waited upon me, while my uncle, sitting in a corner, asked me many questions as to my mother and myself. When my meal was finished, he ordered his man Enoch to unpack my gun. I observed that two other guns, old rusted weapons, were leaning against the wall beside the window.

"It's the window I'm afraid of," said my uncle, in the deep, reverberant voice which contrasted oddly with his plump little figure. "The door's safe against anythin', short of dynamite, but the window's a terror. Hi! Hi!" he yelled, "don't walk across the light! You can duck when you pass the lattice."

"For fear of being seen?" I asked.

"For fear of bein' shot, my lad. That's the trouble. Now, come an' sit beside me on the trestle 'ere, and I'll tell you all about it, for I can see that you are the right sort and can be trusted."

His flattery was clumsy and halting, and it was evident that he was very eager to conciliate me. I sat down beside him, and he drew a folded paper from his pocket. It was a Western *Morning News,* and the date was ten days before. The passage over which he pressed a long, black nail was concerned with the release from Dartmoor of a convict named Elias, whose term of sentence had been remitted on account of his defence of a warder who had been attacked in the quarries. The whole account was only a few lines long.

"Who is he, then?" I asked.

My uncle cocked his distorted foot into the air. "That's 'is mark!" said he. "'E was doin' time for that. Now 'e's out an' after me again."

"But why should he be after you?"

"Because 'e wants to kill me. Because 'e'll never rest, the worrying devil, until 'e 'as 'ad 'is revenge on me. It's this way, nephew! I've no secrets from you. 'E thinks I've wronged 'im. For argument's sake we'll suppose I 'ave wronged 'im. And now 'im and 'is friends are after me."

"Who are his friends?"

My uncle's boom sank suddenly to a frightened whisper. "Sailors!" said he. "I knew they would come when I saw that 'ere paper, and two days ago I looked through that window and three of them was standin' lookin' at the 'ouse. It was after that that I wrote to your mother. They've marked me down, and they're waitin' for 'im."

"But why not send for the police?"

My uncle's eyes avoided mine.

"Police are no use," said he. "It's you that can help me."

"What can I do?"

"I'll tell you. I'm going to move. That's what all these boxes are for. Everything will soon be packed and ready. I 'ave friends at Leeds, and I shall be safer there. Not safe, mind you, but safer. I start tomorrow evening, and if you will stand by me until then I will make it worth your while. There's only Enoch and me to do everything, but we shall 'ave it all ready, I promise you, by tomorrow evening. The cart will be round then, and you and me and Enoch and the boy William can guard the things as far as Congleton station. Did you see anything of them on the fells?"

"Yes," said I, "a sailor stopped us on the way."

"Ah, I knew they were watching us. That was why I asked you to get out at the wrong station and to drive to Purcell's instead of comin' 'ere. We are blockaded—that's the word."

"And there was another," said I, "a man with a pipe."

"What was 'e like?"

"Thin face, freckles, a peaked—"

My uncle gave a hoarse scream.

"That's 'im! that's 'im! 'e's come! God be merciful to me, a sinner!" He went click-clacking about the room with his great foot like one distracted. There was something piteous and baby-like in that big, bald head, and for the first time I felt a gush of pity for him.

"Come, uncle," said I, "you are living in a civilized land. There is a law that will bring these gentry to order. Let me drive over to the county police-station tomorrow morning and I'll soon set things right."

But he shook his head at me.

"'E's cunning and 'e's cruel," said he. "I can't draw a breath without thinking of him, cos 'e buckled up three of my ribs. 'E'll kill me this time, sure. There's only one chance. We must leave what we 'ave not packed, and we must be off first thing tomorrow mornin'. Great God, what's that!"

A tremendous knock upon the door had reverberated through the house and then another and another. An iron fist seemed to be beating upon it. My uncle collapsed into his chair. I seized a gun and ran to the door.

"Who's there?" I shouted.

There was no answer.

I opened the shutter and looked out.

No one was there.

And then suddenly I saw that a long slip of paper was protruding through the slit of the door. I held it to the light. In rude but vigorous handwriting the message ran:—

"Put them out on the doorstep and save your skin."

"What do they want?" I asked, as I read him the message.

"What they'll never 'ave! No, by the Lord, never!" he cried, with a fine burst of spirit. "'Ere, Enoch! Enoch!"

The old fellow came running to the call.

"Enoch, I've been a good master to you all my life, and it's your turn now. Will you take a risk for me?"

I thought better of my uncle when I saw how readily the man consented. Whomever else he had wronged, this one at least seemed to love him.

"Put your cloak on and your 'at, Enoch, and out with you by the back door. You know the way across the moor to the Purcells'. Tell them that I must 'ave the cart first thing in the mornin', and that Purcell must come with the shepherd as well. We must get clear of this or we are done. First thing in the mornin', Enoch, and ten pound for the job. Keep the black cloak on and move slow, and they will never see you. We'll keep the 'ouse till you come back."

It was a job for a brave man to venture out into the vague and invisible dangers of the fell, but the old servant took it as the most ordinary of messages. Picking his long, black cloak and his soft hat from the hook behind the door, he was ready on the instant. We extinguished the small lamp in the back passage, softly unbarred the back door, slipped him out, and barred it up again. Looking through the small hall window, I saw his black garments merge instantly into the night.

"It is but a few hours before the light comes, nephew," said my uncle, after he had tried all the bolts and bars. "You shall never regret this night's work. If we come through safely it will be the making of you. Stand by me till mornin', and I stand by you while there's breath in my body. The cart will be 'ere by five. What isn't ready we can afford to leave be'ind. We've only to load up and make for the early train at Congleton."

"Will they let us pass?"

"In broad daylight they dare not stop us. There will be six of us, if they all come, and three guns. We can fight our way through. Where can they get guns, common, wandering seamen? A pistol or two at the most. If we can keep them out for a few hours we are safe. Enoch must be 'alfway to Purcell's by now."

"But what do these sailors want?" I repeated. "You say yourself that you wronged them."

A look of mulish obstinacy came over his large, white face.

"Don't ask questions, nephew, and just do what I ask you," said he. "Enoch won't come back. 'E'll just bide there and come with the cart. 'Ark, what is that?"

A distant cry rang from out of the darkness, and then another one, short and sharp like the wail of the curlew.

"It's Enoch!" said my uncle, gripping my arm. "They're killin' poor old Enoch."

The cry came again, much nearer, and I heard the sound of hurrying steps and a shrill call for help.

"They are after 'im!" cried my uncle, rushing to the front door. He picked up the lantern and flashed it through the little shutter. Up the yellow funnel of light a man was running frantically, his head bowed and a black cloak fluttering behind him. The moor seemed to be alive with dim pursuers.

"The bolt! The bolt!" gasped my uncle. He pushed it back whilst I turned the key, and we swung the door open to admit the fugitive. He dashed in and turned at once with a long yell of triumph. "Come on, lads! Tumble up, all hands, tumble up! Smartly there, all of you!"

It was so quickly and neatly done that we were taken by storm before we knew that we were attacked. The passage was full of rushing sailors. I slipped out of the clutch of one and ran for my gun, but it was only to crash down on to the stone floor an instant later with two of them holding on to me. They were so deft and quick that my hands were lashed together even while I struggled, and I was dragged into the settle corner, unhurt but very sore in spirit at the cunning with which our defences had been forced and the ease with which we had been overcome. They had not even troubled to bind my uncle, but he had been pushed into his chair, and the guns had been taken away. He sat with a very white face, his homely figure and absurd row of curls looking curiously out of place among the wild figures who surrounded him.

"There were six of them, all evidently sailors. One I recognized as the man with the earrings whom I had already met upon the road that evening They were all fine, weather-bronzed, bewhiskered fellows. In the midst of them, leaning against the table, was the freckled man who had passed me on the moor. The great black cloak which poor Enoch had taken out with him was still hanging from his shoulders. He was of a very different type from the others—crafty, cruel, dangerous, with sly, thoughtful eyes which gloated over my uncle. They suddenly turned themselves upon me and I never knew how one's skin can creep at a man's glance before.

"Who are you?" he asked. "Speak out, or we'll find a way to make you."

"I am Mr. Stephen Maple's nephew, come to visit him."

"You are, are you? Well, I wish you joy of your uncle and of your visit too. Quick's the word, lads, for we must be aboard before morning. What shall we do with the old 'un?"

"Trice him up Yankee fashion and give him six dozen," said one of the seamen.

"D'you hear, you cursed Cockney thief? We'll beat the life out of you if you don't give back what you've stolen. Where are they? I know you never parted with them."

My uncle pursed up his lips and shook his head, with a face in which his fear and his obstinacy contended.

"Won't tell, won't you? We'll see about that! Get him ready, Jim!"

One of the seamen seized my uncle, and pulled his coat and shirt over his shoulders. He sat lumped in his chair, his body all creased into white rolls which shivered with cold and with terror.

"Up with him to those hooks."

There were rows of them along the walls where the smoked meat used to be hung. The seamen tied my uncle by the wrists to two of these. Then one of them undid his leather belt.

"The buckle end, Jim," said the captain. "Give him the buckle."

"You cowards," I cried; "to beat an old man!"

"We'll beat a young one next," said he, with a malevolent glance at my corner. "Now, Jim, cut a wad out of him!"

"Give him one more chance!" cried one of the seamen.

"Aye, aye," growled one or two others. "Give the swab a chance!"

"If you turn soft, you may give them up for ever," said the captain. "One thing or the other! You must lash it out of him; or you may give up what you took such pains to win and what would make you gentlemen for life—every man of you. There's nothing else for it. Which shall it be?"

"Let him have it," they cried, savagely.

"Then stand clear!" The buckle of the man's belt whined savagely as he whirled it over his shoulder.

But my uncle cried out before the blow fell.

"I can't stand it!" he cried. "Let me down!"

"Where are they, then?"

"I'll show you if you'll let me down."

They cast off the handkerchiefs and he pulled his coat over his fat, round shoulders. The seamen stood round him, the most intense curiosity and excitement upon their swarthy faces.

"No gammon!" cried the man with the freckles. "We'll kill you joint by joint if you try to fool us. Now then! Where are they?"

"In my bedroom."

"Where is that?"

"The room above."

"Whereabouts?"

"In the corner of the oak ark by the bed."

The seamen all rushed to the stair, but the captain called them back.

"We don't leave this cunning old fox behind us. Ha, your face drops at that, does it? By the Lord, I believe you are trying to slip your anchor. Here, lads, make him fast and take him along!"

With a confused trampling of feet they rushed up the stairs, dragging my uncle in the midst of them. For an instant I was alone. My hands were tied but not my feet. If I could find my way across the moor I might rouse the police and intercept these rascals before they could reach the sea. For a moment I hesitated as to whether I should leave my uncle alone in such a plight. But I should be of more service to him—or, at the worst, to his property—if I went than if I stayed. I rushed to the hall door, and as I reached it I heard a yell above my head, a shattering, splintering noise, and then amid a chorus of shouts a huge weight fell with a horrible thud at my very feet. Never while I live will that squelching thud pass out of my ears. And there, just in front of me, in the lane of light cast by the open door, lay my unhappy uncle, his bald head twisted on to one shoulder, like the wrung neck of a chicken. It needed but a glance to see that his spine was broken and that he was dead.

The gang of seamen had rushed downstairs so quickly that they were clustered at the door and crowding all round me almost as soon as I had realized what had occurred.

"It's no doing of ours, mate," said one of them to me. "He hove himself through the window, and that's the truth. Don't you put it down to us."

"He thought he could get to windward of us if once he was out in the dark, you see," said another. "But he came head foremost and broke his bloomin' neck."

"And a blessed good job too!" cried the chief, with a savage oath. "I'd have done it for him if he hadn't took the lead. Don't make any mistake, my lads, this is murder, and we're all in it together. There's only one way out of it, and that is to hang together, unless, as the saying goes, you mean to hang apart. There's only one witness—"

He looked at me with his malicious little eyes, and I saw that he had something that gleamed—either a knife or a revolver—in the breast of his pea-jacket. Two of the men slipped between us.

"Stow that, Captain Elias," said one of them. "If this old man met his end, it is through no fault of ours. The worst we ever meant him was to take some of the skin off his back. But as to this young fellow, we have no quarrel with him—"

"You fool, you may have no quarrel with him, but he has his quarrel with you. He'll swear your life away if you don't silence his tongue. It's his life or ours, and don't you make any mistake."

"Aye, aye, the skipper has the longest head of any of us. Better do what he tells you," cried another.

But my champion, who was the fellow with the earrings, covered me with his own broad chest and swore roundly that no one should lay a finger on me. The others were equally divided, and my fate might have been the cause of a quarrel between them when suddenly the captain gave a cry of delight and amazement which was taken up by the whole gang. I followed their eyes and outstretched fingers, and this was what I saw.

My uncle was lying with his legs outstretched, and the club foot was that which was furthest from us. All round this foot a dozen brilliant objects were twinkling and flashing in the yellow light which streamed from the open door. The captain caught up the lantern and held it to the place. The huge sole of his boot had been shattered in the fall, and it was clear now that it had been a hollow box in which he stowed his valuables, for the path was all sprinkled with precious stones. Three which I saw were of an unusual size, and as many as forty, I should think, of fair value. The seamen had cast themselves down and were greedily gathering them up, when my friend with the earrings plucked me by the sleeve.

"Here's your chance, mate," he whispered. "Off you go before worse comes of it."

It was a timely hint, and it did not take me long to act upon it. A few cautious steps and I had passed unobserved beyond the circle of light. Then I set off running, falling and rising and falling again, for no one who has not tried it can tell how hard it is to run over uneven ground with hands which are fastened together. I ran and ran, until for want of breath I could no longer put one foot before the other. But I need not have hurried so, for when I had gone a long way I stopped at last to breathe, and, looking back, I could still see the gleam of the lantern far away, and the outline of the seamen who squatted round it. Then at last this single point of light went suddenly out, and the whole great moor was left in the thickest darkness.

So deftly was I tied, that it took me a long half-hour and a broken tooth before I got my hands free. My idea

was to make my way across to the Purcells' farm, but north
was the same as south under that pitchy sky, and for hours
I wandered among the rustling, scuttling sheep without
any certainty as to where I was going. When at last there
came a glimmer in the east, and the undulating fells, grey
with the morning mist, rolled once more to the horizon, I
recognized that I was close by Purcell's farm, and there a
little in front of me I was startled to see another man walking in the same direction. At first I approached him warily,
but before I overtook him I knew by the bent back and
tottering step that it was Enoch, the old servant, and right
glad I was to see that he was living. He had been knocked
down, beaten, and his cloak and hat taken away by these
ruffians, and all night he had wandered in the darkness,
like myself, in search of help. He burst into tears when I
told him of his master's death, and sat hiccoughing with
the hard, dry sobs of an old man among the stones upon
the moor.

"It's the men of the *Black Mogul*," he said. "Yes, yes,
I knew that they would be the end of 'im."

"Who are they?" I asked.

"Well, well, you are one of 'is own folk," said he. "'E
'as passed away; yes, yes, it is all over and done. I can tell
you about it, no man better, but mum's the word with old
Enoch unless master wants 'im to speak. But his own
nephew who came to 'elp 'im in the hour of need—yes,
yes, Mister John, you ought to know.

"It was like this, sir. Your uncle 'ad 'is grocer's business at Stepney, but 'e 'ad another business also. 'E would
buy as well as sell, and when 'e bought 'e never asked no

questions where the stuff came from. Why should 'e? It wasn't no business of 'is, was it? If folk brought him a stone or a silver plate, what was it to 'im where they got it? That's good sense, and it ought to be good law, as I 'old. Any'ow, it was good enough for us at Stepney

"Well, there was a steamer came from South Africa what foundered at sea. At least, they say so, and Lloyd's paid the money. She 'ad some very fine diamonds invoiced as being aboard of 'er. Soon after, there came the brig *Black Mogul* into the port o' London, with 'er papers all right as 'avin' cleared from Port Elizabeth with a cargo of 'ides. The captain, which 'is name was Elias, 'e came to see the master, and what d'you think that 'e 'ad to sell? Why, sir, as I'm a livin' sinner 'e 'ad a packet of diamonds for all the world just the same as what was lost out o' that there African steamer. 'Ow did 'e get them? I don't know. Master didn't know. 'E didn't seek to know either. The captain, 'e was anxious for reasons of 'is own to get them safe, so 'e gave them to master, same as you might put a thing in a bank. But master 'e'd 'ad time to get fond of them, and 'e wasn't over satisfied as to where the *Black Mogul* 'ad been tradin', or where her captain 'ad got the stones, so when 'e come back for them, the master 'e said as 'e thought they were best in 'is own 'ands. Mind, I don't 'old with it myself, but that was what master said to Captain Elias in the little back parlour at Stepney. That was 'ow 'e got 'is leg broke and three of his ribs.

"So the captain got jugged for that, and the master, when 'e was able to get about, thought that 'e would 'ave peace for fifteen years, and 'e came away from London because 'e was afraid of the sailor men; but, at the end of five years, the captain was out and after 'im, with as many of 'is crew as 'e could gather. Send for the perlice, you says! Well, there are two sides to that, and the master, 'e wasn't much more fond of the perlice than Elias was. But they fair 'emmed master in, as you 'ave seen for yourself, and they bested 'im at last, and the loneliness that 'e thought would be 'is safety 'as proved 'is ruin. Well, well, 'e was 'ard to many, but a good master to me, and it's long before I come on such another."

One word in conclusion. A strange cutter, which had been hanging about the coast, was seen to beat down the Irish Sea that morning, and it is conjectured that Elias and his men were on board of it. At any rate, nothing has been heard of them since. It was shown at the inquest that my uncle had lived in a sordid fashion for years, and he left little behind him. The mere knowledge that he possessed this treasure, which he carried about with him in so extraordinary a fashion, had appeared to be the joy of his life, and he had never, as far as we could learn, tried to realize any of his diamonds. So his disreputable name when living was not atoned for by any posthumous benevolence, and the family, equally scandalized by his life and by his death, have finally buried all memory of the club-footed grocer of Stepney.

/ The Sealed Room /

A solicitor of an active habit and athletic tastes who is compelled by his hopes of business to remain within the four walls of his office from ten till five must take what exercise he can in the evenings. Hence it was that I was in the habit of indulging in very long nocturnal excursions, in which I sought the heights of Hampstead and Highgate in order to cleanse my system from the impure air of Abchurch Lane. It was in the course of one of these aimless rambles that I first met Felix Stanniford, and so led up to what has been the most extraordinary adventure of my lifetime.

One evening—it was in April or early May of the year 1894—I made my way to the extreme northern fringe of London, and was walking down one of those fine avenues of high brick villas which the huge city is forever pushing farther and farther out into the country. It was a fine, clear spring night, the moon was shining out of an unclouded sky, and I, having already left many miles behind me, was inclined to walk slowly and look about me. In this contemplative mood, my attention was arrested by one of the houses which I was passing.

It was a very large building, standing in its grounds, a little back from the road. It was modern in appearance, and yet it was far less so than its neighbours, all of which were crudely and painfully new. Their symmetrical line was broken by the gap caused by the laurel-studded lawn, with the great, dark, gloomy house looming at the back of it. Evidently it had been the country retreat of some wealthy merchant, built perhaps when the nearest street was a mile off, and now gradually overtaken and surrounded by the red brick tentacles of the London octopus. The next stage, I reflected, would be its digestion and absorption, so that the cheap builder might rear a dozen eighty-pound-a-year villas upon the garden frontage. And then, as all this passed vaguely through my mind, an incident occurred which brought my thoughts into quite another channel.

A four-wheeled cab, that opprobrium of London, was coming jolting and creaking in one direction, while in the other there was a yellow glare from the lamp of a cyclist. They were the only moving objects in the whole long, moonlit road, and yet they crashed into each other with that malignant accuracy which brings two ocean liners together in the broad waste of the Atlantic. It was the cyclist's fault. He tried to cross in front of the cab, miscalculated his distance, and was knocked sprawling by the horse's shoulder. He rose, snarling; the cabman swore back at him, and then, realizing that his number had not yet been taken, lashed his horse and lumbered off. The cyclist caught at the handles of his prostrate machine, and then suddenly sat down with a groan. "Oh, Lord!" he said.

I ran across the road to his side. "Any harm done?" I asked,

"It's my ankle," said he. "Only a twist, I think; but it's pretty painful. Just give me your hand, will you?"

He lay in the yellow circle of the cycle lamp, and I noted as I helped him to his feet that he was a gentlemanly young fellow, with a slight dark moustache and large, brown eyes, sensitive and nervous in appearance, with indications of weak health upon his sunken cheeks. Work or worry had left its traces upon his thin, yellow face. He stood up when I pulled his hand, but he held one foot in the air, and he groaned as he moved it.

"I can't put it to the ground," said he.

"Where do you live?"

"Here!" He nodded his head towards the big, dark house in the garden. "I was cutting across to the gate when that confounded cab ran into me. Could you help me so far?"

It was easily done. I put his cycle inside the gate, and then I supported him down the drive, and up the steps to the hall door. There was not a light anywhere, and the place was as black and silent as if no one had ever lived in it.

"That will do. Thank you very much," said he, fumbling with his key in the lock.

"No, you must allow me to see you safe."

He made some feeble, petulant protest, and then realized that he could really do nothing without me. The door had opened into a pitch-dark hall. He lurched forward, with my hand still on his arm.

"This door to the right," said he, feeling about in the darkness.

I opened the door, and at the same moment he managed to strike a light. There was a lamp upon the table, and we lit it between us. "Now, I'm all right. You can leave me now! Good-bye!" said he, and with the words he sat down in the armchair and fainted dead away.

It was a queer position for me. The fellow looked so ghastly, that really I was not sure that he was not dead. Presently his lips quivered and his breast heaved, but his eyes were two white slits and his colour was horrible. The responsibility was more than I could stand. I pulled at the bell-rope, and heard the bell ringing furiously far away. But no one came in response. The bell tinkled away into silence, which no murmur or movement came to break. I waited, and rang again, with the same result. There must be someone about. This young gentleman could not live all alone in that huge house. His people ought to know of his condition. If they would not answer the bell, I must hunt them out myself. I seized the lamp and rushed from the room.

What I saw outside amazed me. The hall was empty. The stairs were bare, and yellow with dust. There were three doors opening into spacious rooms, and each was uncarpeted and undraped, save for the grey webs which drooped from the cornice, and rosettes of lichen which had formed upon the walls. My feet reverberated in those empty and silent chambers. Then I wandered on down the passage, with the idea that the kitchens, at least, might be tenanted. Some caretaker might lurk in some secluded room. No, they were all equally desolate. Despairing of finding any help, I ran down another corridor, and came on something which surprised me more than ever.

The passage ended in a large, brown door, and the door had a seal of red wax the size of a five-shilling piece over the keyhole. This seal gave me the impression of having been there for a long time, for it was dusty and discoloured. I was still staring at it, and wondering what that door might conceal, when I heard a voice calling behind me, and, running back, found my young man sitting up in his chair and very much astonished at finding himself in darkness.

"Why on earth did you take the lamp away?" he asked.

"I was looking for assistance."

"You might look for some time," said he. "I am alone in the house."

"Awkward if you get an illness."

"It was foolish of me to faint. I inherit a weak heart from my mother, and pain or emotion has that effect upon me. It will carry me off some day, as it did her. You're not a doctor, are you?"

"No, a lawyer. Frank Alder is my name."

"Mine is Felix Stanniford. Funny that I should meet a lawyer, for my friend, Mr. Perceval, was saying that we should need one soon."

"Very happy, I am sure."

"Well, that will depend upon him, you know. Did you say that you had run with that lamp all over the ground floor?"

"Yes."

"*All* over it?" he asked, with emphasis, and he looked at me very hard.

"I think so. I kept on hoping that I should find someone."

"Did you enter all the rooms?" he asked, with the same intent gaze.

"Well, all that I could enter."

"Oh, then you *did* notice it!" said he, and he shrugged his shoulders with the air of a man who makes the best of a bad job.

"Notice what?"

"Why, the door with the seal on it."

"Yes, I did."

"Weren't you curious to know what was in it?"

"Well, it did strike me as unusual."

"Do you think you could go on living alone in this house, year after year, just longing all the time to know what is at the other side of that door, and yet not looking?"

"Do you mean to say," I cried, "that you don't know yourself?"

"No more than you do."

"Then why don't you look?"

"I mustn't," said he.

He spoke in a constrained way, and I saw that I had blundered on to some delicate ground. I don't know that I am more inquisitive than my neighbours, but there certainly was something in the situation which appealed very strongly to my curiosity. However, my last excuse for re-

maining in the house was gone now that my companion
had recovered his senses, I rose to go.

"Are you in a hurry?" he asked.

"No; I have nothing to do."

"Well, I should be very glad if you would stay with me
a little. The fact is that I live a retired and secluded life
here. I don't suppose there is a man in London who leads
such a life as I do. It is quite unusual for me to have any
one to talk with."

I looked round at the little room, scantily furnished,
with a sofa-bed at one side. Then I thought of the great,
bare house, and the sinister door with the discoloured red
seal upon it. There was something queer and grotesque in
the situation, which made me long to know a little more.
Perhaps I should, if I waited. I told him that I should be
very happy.

"You will find the spirits and a siphon upon the side
table. Yon must forgive me if I cannot act as host, but I
can't get across the room. Those are cigars in the tray there.
I'll take one myself, I think. And so you are a solicitor, Mr.
Alder?"

"Yes."

"And I am nothing. I am that most helpless of living
creatures, the son of a millionaire. I was brought up with
the expectation of great wealth; and here I am, a poor man,
without any profession at all. And then, on the top of it all,
I am left with this great mansion on my hands, which I
cannot possibly keep up. Isn't it an absurd situation? For
me to use this as my dwelling is like a coster drawing his

barrow with a thoroughbred. A donkey would be more useful to him, and a cottage to me."

"But why not sell the house?" I asked.

"I mustn't."

"Let it, then?"

"No, I mustn't do that either."

I looked puzzled, and my companion smiled.

"I'll tell you how it is, if it won't bore you," said he.

"On the contrary, I should be exceedingly interested."

"I think, after your kind attention to me, I cannot do less than relieve any curiosity that you may feel. You must know that my father was Stanislaus Stanniford, the banker."

Stanniford, the banker! I remembered the name at once. His flight from the country some seven years before had been one of the scandals and sensations of the time.

"I see that you remember," said my companion. "My poor father left the country to avoid numerous friends, whose savings he had invested in an unsuccessful speculation. He was a nervous, sensitive man, and the responsibility quite upset his reason. He had committed no legal offence. It was purely a matter of sentiment. He would not even face his own family, and he died among strangers without ever letting us know where he was."

"He died!" said I.

"We could not prove his death, but we know that it must be so, because the speculations came right again, and so there was no reason why he should not look any man in the face. He would have returned if he were alive. But he must have died in the last two years."

"Why in the last two years?"

"Because we heard from him two years ago."

"Did he not tell you then where he was living?"

"The letter came from Paris, but no address was given. It was when my poor mother died. He wrote to me then, with some instructions and some advice, and I have never heard from him since."

"Had you heard before?"

"Oh, yes, we had heard before, and that's where our mystery of the sealed door, upon which you stumbled to-night, has its origin. Pass me that desk, if you please. Here I have my father's letters, and you are the first man except Mr. Perceval who has seen them."

"Who is Mr. Perceval, may I ask?"

"He was my father's confidential clerk, and he has continued to be the friend and adviser of my mother and then of myself. I don't know what we should have done without Perceval. He saw the letters, but no one else. This is the first one, which came on the very day when my father fled, seven years ago. Read it to yourself."

This is the letter which I read:—

"My Ever Dearest Wife,—

"Since Sir William told me how weak your heart is, and how harmful any shock might be, I have never talked about my business affairs to you. The time has come when at all risks I can no longer refrain from telling you that things have been going badly with me. This will cause me to leave you for a little time, but it is with the absolute assurance that we shall see each other very soon. On this you can thoroughly rely. Our parting is only for a very short time, my own darling, so don't let it fret you, and above all don't let it impair your health, for that is what I want above all things to avoid.

"Now, I have a request to make, and I implore you by all that binds us together to fulfil it exactly as I tell you. There are some things which I do not wish to be seen by anyone in my dark room—the room which I use for photographic purposes at the end of the garden passage. To prevent any painful thoughts, I may assure you once for all, dear, that it is nothing of which I need be ashamed. But still I do not wish you or Felix to enter that room. It is locked, and I implore you when you receive this to at once place a seal over the lock, and leave it so. Do not sell or let the house, for in either case my secret will be discovered. As long as you or Felix are in the house, I know that you will comply with my wishes. When Felix is twenty-one he may enter the room—not before.

"And now, good-bye, my own best of wives. During our short separation you can consult Mr. Perceval on any matters which may arise. He has my complete confidence. I hate to leave Felix and you—even for a time—but there is really no choice.

"Ever and always your loving husband,

"Stanislaus Stanniford.

"June 4th, 1887."

"These are very private family matters for me to in-flict upon you," said my companion, apologetically. "You must look upon it as done in your professional capacity. I have wanted to speak about it for years."

"I am honoured by your confidence," I answered, "and exceedingly interested by the facts."

"My father was a man who was noted for his almost morbid love of truth. He was always pedantically accu-rate. When he said, therefore, that he hoped to see my mother very soon, and when he said that he had nothing to be ashamed of in that dark room, you may rely upon it that he meant it."

"Then what can it be?" I ejaculated.

"Neither my mother nor I could imagine. We carried out his wishes to the letter, and placed the seal upon the door; there it has been ever since. My mother lived for five years after my father's disappearance, although at the time all the doctors said that she could not survive long. Her heart was terribly diseased. During the first few months she had two letters from my father. Both had the Paris post-mark, but no address. They were short and to the same effect: that they would soon be re-united, and that she should not fret. Then there was a silence, which lasted until her death; and then came a letter to me of so private a nature that I cannot show it to you, begging me never to think evil of him, giving me much good advice, and say-ing that the sealing of the room was of less importance now than during the lifetime of my mother, but that the opening might still cause pain to others, and that, there-fore, he thought it best that it should be postponed until my twenty-first year, for the lapse of time would make things easier. In the meantime, he committed the care of the room to me; so now you can understand how it is that, although I am a very poor man, I can neither let nor sell this great house."

"You could mortgage it."

"My father had already done so."

"It is a most singular state of affairs."

"My mother and I were gradually compelled to sell the furniture and to dismiss the servants, until now, as you see, I am living unattended in a single room. But I have only two more months."

"What do you mean?"

"Why, that in two months I come of age. The first thing that I do will be to open that door; the second, to get rid of the house."

"Why should your father have continued to stay away when these investments had recovered themselves?"

"He must be dead."

"You say that he had not committed any legal offence when he fled the country?"

"None."

"Why should he not take your mother with him?"

"I do not know."

"Why should he conceal his address?"

"I do not know."

"Why should he allow your mother to die and be buried without coming back?"

"I do not know."

"My dear sir," said I, "if I may speak with the frankness of a professional adviser, I should say that it is very clear that your father had the strongest reasons for keeping out of the country, and that, if nothing has been proved against him, he at least thought that something might be, and refused to put himself within the power of the law. Surely that must be obvious, for in what other possible way can the facts be explained?"

My companion did not take my suggestion in good part.

"You had not the advantage of knowing my father, Mr. Alder," he said, coldly. "I was only a boy when he left us, but I shall always look upon him as my ideal man. His only fault was that he was too sensitive and too unselfish. That anyone should lose money through him would cut him to the heart. His sense of honour was most acute, and any theory of his disappearance which conflicts with that is a mistaken one."

It pleased me to hear the lad speak out so roundly, and yet I knew that the facts were against him, and that he was incapable of taking an unprejudiced view of the situation.

"I only speak as an outsider," said I. "And now I must leave you, for I have a long walk before me. Your story has interested me so much that I should be glad if you could let me know the sequel."

"Leave me your card," said he; and so, having bade him "good-night," I left him.

I heard nothing more of the matter for some time, and had almost feared that it would prove to be one of those fleeting experiences which drift away from our direct observation and end only in a hope or a suspicion. One afternoon, however, a card bearing the name of Mr. J. E. Perceval was brought up to my office in Abchurch Lane, and its bearer, a small dry, bright-eyed fellow of fifty, was ushered in by the clerk.

"I believe, sir," said he, "that my name has been mentioned to you by my young friend, Mr. Felix Stanniford?"

"Of course," I answered, "I remember."

"He spoke to you, I understand, about the circumstances in connection with the disappearance of my former employer, Mr. Stanislaus Stanniford, and the existence of a sealed room in his former residence."

"He did."

"And you expressed an interest in the matter."

"It interested me extremely."

"You are aware that we hold Mr. Stanniford's permission to open the door on the twenty-first birthday of his son?"

"I remember."

"The twenty-first birthday is today."

"Have you opened it?" I asked, eagerly.

"Not yet, sir," said he, gravely. "I have reason to believe that it would be well to have witnesses present when that door is opened. You are a lawyer and you are acquainted with the facts. Will you be present on the occasion?"

"Most certainly."

"You are employed during the day, and so am I. Shall we meet at nine o'clock at the house?"

"I will come with pleasure."

"Then you will find us waiting for you. Good-bye, for the present." He bowed solemnly, and took his leave.

I kept my appointment that evening, with a brain which was weary with fruitless attempts to think out some plausible explanation of the mystery which we were about to solve. Mr. Perceval and my young acquaintance were waiting for me in the little room. I was not surprised to see the young man looking pale and nervous, but I was rather astonished to find the dry little city man in a state of intense, though partially suppressed, excitement. His cheeks were flushed, his hands twitching, and he could not stand still for an instant.

Stanniford greeted me warmly, and thanked me many times for having come. "And now, Perceval," said he to his companion, "I suppose there is no obstacle to our putting the thing through without delay? I shall be glad to get it over."

The banker's clerk took up the lamp and led the way. But he paused in the passage outside the door, and his hand was shaking, so that the light flickered up and down the high, bare walls.

"Mr. Stanniford," said he, in a cracking voice, "I hope you will prepare yourself in case any shock should be awaiting you when that seal is removed and the door is opened."

"What could there be, Perceval? You are trying to frighten me."

"No, Mr. Stanniford; but I should wish you to be ready . . . to be braced up . . . not to allow yourself . . ." He had to lick his dry lips between every jerky sentence, and I suddenly realized, as clearly as if he had told me, that he knew what was behind that closed door, and that it *was* something terrible. "Here are the keys, Mr. Stanniford, but remember my warning!"

He had a bunch of assorted keys in his hand, and the young man snatched them from him. Then he thrust a knife under the discolored red seal and jerked it off. The lamp was rattling and shaking in Perceval's hands, so I took it from him and held it near the keyhole, while Stanniford tried key after key. At last one turned in the lock, the door flew open, he took one step into the room, and then, with a horrible cry, the young man fell senseless at our feet.

If I had not given heed to the clerk's warning, and braced myself for a shock, I should certainly have dropped the lamp. The room, windowless and bare, was fitted up as a photographic laboratory, with a tap and sink at the side of it. A shelf of bottles and measures stood at one side, and a peculiar, heavy smell, partly chemical, partly animal, filled the air. A single table and chair were in front of us, and at this, with his back turned towards us, a man was seated in the act of writing. His outline and attitude were as natural as life; but as the light fell upon him, it made my hair rise to see that the nape of his neck was black and wrinkled, and no thicker than my wrist. Dust lay upon him—thick, yellow dust—upon his hair, his shoulders, his shrivelled, lemon-coloured hands. His head had fallen forward upon his breast. His pen still rested upon a discoloured sheet of paper.

"My poor master! My poor, poor master!" cried the clerk, and the tears were running down his cheeks.

"What!" I cried, "Mr. Stanislaus Stanniford!"

"Here he has sat for seven years. Oh, why would he do it? I begged him, I implored him, I went on my knees to him, but he would have his way. You see the key on the table. He had locked the door upon the inside. And he has written something. We must take it."

"Yes, yes, take it, and for God's sake, let us get out of this," I cried; "the air is poisonous. Come, Stanniford, come!" Taking an arm each, we half led and half carried the terrified man back to his own room.

"It was my father!" he cried, as he recovered his consciousness. "He is sitting there dead in his chair. You knew it, Perceval! This was what you meant when you warned me."

"Yes, I knew it, Mr. Stanniford. I have acted for the best all along, but my position has been a terribly difficult one. For seven years I have known that your father was dead in that room."

"You knew it, and never told us!"

"Don't be harsh with me, Mr. Stanniford, sir! Make allowance for a man who has had a hard part to play."

"My head is swimming round. I cannot grasp it!" He staggered up, and helped himself from the brandy bottle. "These letters to my mother and to myself—were they forgeries?"

"No, sir; your father wrote them and addressed them, and left them in my keeping to be posted. I have followed

his instructions to the very letter in all things. He was my
master, and I have obeyed him."

The brandy had steadied the young man's shaken
nerves. "Tell me about it. I can stand it now," said he.

"Well, Mr. Stanniford, you know that at one time there
came a period of great trouble upon your father, and he
thought that many poor people were about to lose their
savings through his fault. He was a man who was so ten-
der-hearted that he could not bear the thought. It worried
him and tormented him, until he determined to end his
life. Oh, Mr. Stanniford, if you knew how I have prayed
with him and wrestled with him over it, you would never
blame me. And he in turn prayed with me as no man has
ever prayed with me before. He had made up his mind,
and he would do it in any case, he said; but it rested with
me whether his death should be happy and easy or whether
it should be most miserable. I read in his eyes that he meant
what he said. And at last I yielded to his prayers, and I
consented to do his will.

"What was troubling him was this. He had been told
by the first doctor in London that his wife's heart would
fail at the slightest shock. He had a horror of accelerating
her end, and yet his own existence had become unendur-
able to him. How could he end himself without injuring
her?

"You know now the course that he took. He wrote the
letter which she received. There was nothing in it which
was not literally true. When he spoke of seeing her again
so soon, he was referring to her own approaching death,

which he had been assured could not be delayed more than a very few months. So convinced was he of this, that he only left two letters to be forwarded at intervals after his death. She lived five years, and I had no letters to send.

"He left another letter with me to be sent to you, sir, upon the occasion of the death of your mother. I posted all these in Paris to sustain the idea of his being abroad. It was his wish that I should say nothing, and I have said nothing. I have been a faithful servant. Seven years after his death, he thought no doubt that the shock to the feelings of his surviving friends would be lessened. He was always considerate for others."

There was silence for some time. It was broken by young Stanniford.

"I cannot blame you, Perceval. You have spared my mother a shock, which would certainly have broken her heart. What is that paper?"

"It is what your father was writing, sir. Shall I read it to you?"

"Do so."

"'I have taken the poison, and I feel it working in my veins. It is strange, but not painful. When these words are read I shall, if my wishes have been faithfully carried out, have been dead many years. Surely no one who has lost money through me will still bear me animosity. And you, Felix, you will forgive me this family scandal. May God find rest for a sorely wearied spirit!'"

"Amen!" we cried, all three.

/ The Brazilian Cat /

It is hard luck on a young fellow to have expensive tastes, great expectations, aristocratic connections, but no actual money in his pockets and no profession by which he may earn any. The fact was that my father, a good, sanguine, easy-going man, had such confidence in the wealth and benevolence of his bachelor elder brother, Lord Southerton, that he took it for granted that I, his only son, would never be called upon to earn a living for myself. He imagined that if there were not a vacancy for me on the great Southerton Estates, at least there would be found some post in that diplomatic service which still remains the special preserve of our privileged classes. He died too early to realize how false his calculations had been. Neither my uncle nor the State took the slightest notice of me, or showed any interest in my career. An occasional brace of pheasants, or basket of hares, was all that ever reached me to remind me that I was heir to Otwell House and one of the richest estates in the country. In the meantime, I found myself a bachelor and man about town, living in a suite of apartments in Grosvenor Mansions, with no occupation save that of pigeon-shooting and polo-playing at

Hurlingham. Month by month I realized that it was more and more difficult to get the brokers to renew my bills, or to cash any further post obits upon an unentailed property. Ruin lay right across my path, and every day I saw it clearer, nearer, and more absolutely unavoidable.

What made me feel my own poverty the more was that, apart from the great wealth of Lord Southerton, all my other relations were fairly well-to-do. The nearest of these was Everard King, my father's nephew and my own first cousin, who had spent an adventurous life in Brazil, and had now returned to this country to settle down on his fortune. We never knew how he made his money, but he appeared to have plenty of it, for he bought the estate of Greylands, near Clipton-on-the-Marsh, in Suffolk. For the first year of his residence in England he took no more notice of me than my miserly uncle; but at last one summer morning, to my very great relief and joy, I received a letter asking me to come down that very day and spend a short visit at Greylands Court. I was expecting a rather long visit to Bankruptcy Court at the time, and this interruption seemed almost providential. If I could only get on terms with this unknown relative of mine, I might pull through yet. For the family credit, he could not let me go entirely to the wall. I ordered my valet to pack my valise, and I set off the same evening for Clipton-on-the-Marsh.

After changing at Ipswich, a little local train deposited me at a small, deserted station lying amidst a rolling grassy country, with a sluggish and winding river curving in and out amidst the valleys, between high, silted banks, which showed that we were within reach of the tide. No carriage was awaiting me (I found afterwards that my telegram had been delayed), so I hired a dog-cart at the local inn. The driver, an excellent fellow, was full of my relative's praises, and I learned from him that Mr. Everard King was already a name to conjure with in that part of the country. He had entertained the schoolchildren, he had thrown his grounds open to visitors, he had subscribed to charities—in short, his benevolence had been so universal that my driver could only account for it on the supposition that he had Parliamentary ambitions.

My attention was drawn away from my driver's panegyric by the appearance of a very beautiful bird which settled on a telegraph-post beside the road. At first I thought that it was a jay, but it was larger, with a brighter plumage. The driver accounted for its presence at once by saying that it belonged to the very man whom we were about to visit. It seems that the acclimatization of foreign creatures was one of his hobbies, and that he had brought with him from Brazil a number of birds and beasts which he was endeavouring to rear in England. When once we had passed the gates of Greyland's Park, we had ample evidence of this taste of his. Some small spotted deer, a curious wild pig known, I believe, as a peccary, a gorgeously feathered oriole, some sort of armadillo, and a singular lumbering intoed beast like a very fat badger, were among the creatures which I observed as we drove along the winding avenue.

Mr. Everard King, my unknown cousin, was standing in person upon the steps of his house, for he had seen us in the distance, and guessed that it was I. His appearance was very homely and benevolent, short and stout, forty-five years old perhaps, with a round, good-humoured face, burned brown with the tropical sun, and shot with a thousand wrinkles. He wore white linen clothes, in true planter style, with a cigar between his lips, and a large Panama hat upon the back of his head. It was such a figure as one associates with a verandahed bungalow, and it looked curiously out of place in front of this broad, stone English mansion, with its solid wings and its Palladio pillars before the doorway.

"My dear!" he cried, glancing over his shoulder; "my dear, here is our guest! Welcome, welcome to Greylands! I am delighted to make your acquaintance, Cousin Marshall, and I take it as a great compliment that you should honour this sleepy little country place with your presence."

Nothing could be more hearty than his manner, and he set me at my ease in an instant. But it needed all his cordiality to atone for the frigidity and even rudeness of his wife, a tall, haggard woman, who came forward at his summons. She was, I believe, of Brazilian extraction, though she spoke excellent English, and I excused her manners on the score of her ignorance of our customs. She did not attempt to conceal, however, either then or afterwards, that I was not very welcome visitor at Greylands Court. Her actual words were, as a rule, courteous, but she was the possessor of a pair of particularly expressive dark eyes, and I read in them very clearly from the first that she heartily wished me back in London once more.

However, my debts were too pressing and my designs upon my wealthy relative were too vital for me to allow them to be upset by the ill-temper of his wife, so I disregarded her coldness and reciprocated the extreme cordiality of his welcome. No pains had been spared by him to make me comfortable. My room was a charming one. He implored me to tell him anything which could add to my happiness. It was on the tip of my tongue to inform him that a blank cheque would materially help towards that end, but I felt that it might be premature in the present state of our acquaintance. The dinner was excellent, and as we sat together afterwards over his Havanas and coffee, which latter he told me was specially prepared upon his own plantation, it seemed to me that all my driver's eulogies were justified, and that I had never met a more large-hearted and hospitable man.

But, in spite of his cheery good nature, he was a man with a strong will and a fiery temper of his own. Of this I had an example upon the following morning. The curious aversion which Mrs. Everard King had conceived towards me was so strong, that her manner at breakfast was almost offensive. But her meaning became unmistakable when her husband had quitted the room.

"The best train in the day is at twelve-fifteen," said she.

"But I was not thinking of going today," I answered, frankly—perhaps even defiantly, for I was determined not to be driven out by this woman.

"Oh, if it rests with you," said she, and stopped, with a most insolent expression in her eyes.

"I am sure," I answered, "that Mr. Everard King would tell me if I were outstaying my welcome."

"What's this? What's this?" said a voice, and there he was in the room. He had overheard my last words, and a glance at our faces had told him the rest. In an instant his chubby, cheery face set into an expression of absolute ferocity.

"Might I trouble you to walk outside, Marshall," said he. (I may mention that my own name is Marshall King.)

He closed the door behind me, and then, for an instant, I heard him talking in a low voice of concentrated passion to his wife. This gross breach of hospitality had evidently hit upon his tenderest point. I am no eavesdropper, so I walked out on to the lawn. Presently I heard a hurried step behind me, and there was the lady, her face pale with excitement, and her eyes red with tears.

"My husband has asked me to apologize to you, Mr. Marshall King," said she, standing with downcast eyes before me.

"Please do not say another word, Mrs. King."

Her dark eyes suddenly blazed out at me.

"You fool!" she hissed, with frantic vehemence, and turning on her heel swept back to the house.

The insult was so outrageous, so insufferable, that I could only stand staring after her in bewilderment. I was still there when my host joined me. He was his cheery, chubby self once more.

"I hope that my wife has apologized for her foolish remark," said he.

"Oh, yes—yes, certainly!"

He put his hand through my arm and walked with me up and down the lawn.

"You must not take it seriously," said he. "It would grieve me inexpressibly if you curtailed your visit by one hour. The fact is—there is no reason why there should be any concealment between relatives—that my poor dear wife is incredibly jealous. She hates that any one—male or female—should for an instant come between us. Her ideal is a desert island and an eternal *tête-à-tête*. That gives you the clue to her actions, which are, I confess, upon this particular point, not very far removed from mania. Tell me that you will think no more of it."

"No, no; certainly not."

"Then light this cigar and come round with me and see my little menagerie."

The whole afternoon was occupied by this inspection, which included all the birds, beasts, and even reptiles which he had imported. Some were free, some in cages, a few actually in the house. He spoke with enthusiasm of his successes and his failures, his births and his deaths, and he would cry out in his delight, like a schoolboy, when, as we walked, some gaudy bird would flutter up from the grass, or some curious beast slink into the cover. Finally, he led me down a corridor which extended from one wing of the house. At the end of this there was a heavy door with a sliding shutter in it, and beside it there projected from the wall an iron handle attached to a wheel and a drum. A line of stout bars extended across the passage.

"I am about to show you the jewel of my collection," said he. "There is only one other specimen in Europe, now that the Rotterdam cub is dead. It is a Brazilian cat."

"But how does that differ from any other cat?"

"You will soon see that," said he, laughing. "Will you kindly draw that shutter and look through?"

I did so, and found that I was gazing into a large, empty room, with stone flags, and small, barred windows upon the farther wall.

In the centre of this room, lying in the middle of a golden patch of sunlight, there was stretched a huge creature, as large as a tiger, but as black and sleek as ebony. It was simply a very enormous and very well-kept black cat, and it cuddled up and basked in that yellow pool of light exactly as a cat would do. It was so graceful, so sinewy, and so gently and smoothly diabolical, that I could not take my eyes from the opening.

"Isn't he splendid?" said my host, enthusiastically.

"Glorious! I never saw such a noble creature."

"Some people call it a black puma, but really it is not a puma at all. That fellow is nearly eleven feet from tail to tip. Four years ago he was a little ball of black fluff, with two yellow eyes staring out of it. He was sold me as a newborn cub up in the wild country at the headwaters of the Rio Negro. They speared his mother to death after she had killed a dozen of them."

"They are ferocious, then?"

"The most absolutely treacherous and blood-thirsty creatures upon earth. You talk about a Brazilian cat to an up-country Indian, and see him get the jumps. They prefer humans to game. This fellow has never tasted living blood yet, but when he does he will be a terror. At present he won't stand anyone but me in his den. Even Baldwin, the groom, dare not go near him. As to me, I am his mother and father in one."

As he spoke he suddenly, to my astonishment, opened the door and slipped in, closing it instantly behind him. At the sound of his voice the huge, lithe creature rose, yawned, and rubbed its round, black head affectionately against his side, while he patted and fondled it.

"Now, Tommy, into your cage!" said he.

The monstrous cat walked over to one side of the room and coiled itself up under a grating. Everard King came out, and taking the iron handle which I have mentioned, he began to turn it. As he did so the line of bars in the corridor began to pass through a slot in the wall and closed up the front of this grating, so as to make an effective cage. When it was in position he opened the door once more and invited me into the room, which was heavy with the pungent, musty smell peculiar to the great carnivore.

"That's how we work it," said he. "We give him the run of the room for exercise, and then at night we put him in his cage. You can let him out by turning the handle from the passage, or you can, as you have seen, coop him up in the same way. No, no, you should not do that!"

I had put my hand between the bars to pat the glossy, heaving flank. He pulled it back, with a serious face.

"I assure you that he is not safe. Don't imagine that because I can take liberties with him anyone else can. He is very exclusive in his friends—aren't you, Tommy? Ah, he hears his lunch coming to him! Don't you, boy?"

A step sounded in the stone-flagged passage, and the creature had sprung to his feet, and was pacing up and down the narrow cage, his yellow eyes gleaming, and his scarlet tongue rippling and quivering over the white line of his jagged teeth. A groom entered with a coarse joint upon a tray, and thrust it through the bars to him. He pounced lightly upon it, carried it off to the corner, and there, holding it between his paws, tore and wrenched at it, raising his bloody muzzle every now and then to look at us. It was a malignant and yet fascinating sight.

"You can't wonder that I am fond of him, can you?" said my host, as we left the room, "especially when you consider that I have had the rearing of him. It was no joke bringing him over from the centre of South America; but here he is safe and sound—and, as I have said, far the most perfect specimen in Europe. The people at the zoo are dying to have him, but I really can't part with him. Now, I think that I have inflicted my hobby upon you long enough, so we cannot do better than follow Tommy's example, and go to our lunch."

My South American relative was so engrossed by his grounds and their curious occupants, that I hardly gave him credit at first for having any interests outside them. That he had some, and pressing ones, was soon borne in upon me by the number of telegrams which he received. They arrived at all hours, and were always opened by him with the utmost eagerness and anxiety upon his face. Sometimes I imagined that it must be the turf, and sometimes the Stock Exchange, but certainly he had some very urgent business going forward which was not transacted upon the Downs of Suffolk. During the six days of my visit, he had never fewer than three or four telegrams a day, and sometimes as many as seven or eight.

I had occupied these six days so well, that by the end of them I had succeeded in getting upon the most cordial terms with my cousin. Every night we had sat up late in the billiard-room, he telling me the most extraordinary stories of his adventures in America—stories so desperate and reckless, that I could hardly associate them with the brown little, chubby man before me. In return, I ventured upon some of my own reminiscences of London life, which interested him so much, that he vowed he would come up to Grosvenor Mansions and stay with me. He was anxious to see the faster side of city life, and certainly, though I say it, he could not have chosen a more competent guide. It was not until the last day of my visit that I ventured to approach that which was on my mind. I told him frankly about my pecuniary difficulties and my impending ruin, and I asked his advice—though I hoped for something more solid. He listened attentively, puffing hard at his cigar.

"But surely," said he, "you are the heir of our relative, Lord Southerton?"

"I have every reason to believe so, but he would never make me any allowance."

"No, no, I have heard of his miserly ways. My poor Marshall, your position has been a very hard one. By the way, have you heard any news of Lord Southerton's health lately?"

"He has always been in a critical condition ever since my childhood."

"Exactly—a creaking hinge, if ever there was one. Your inheritance may be a long way off. Dear me, how awkwardly situated you are!"

"I had some hopes, sir, that you, knowing all the facts, might be inclined to advance—"

"Don't say another word, my dear boy," he cried, with the utmost cordiality; "we shall talk it over tonight, and I give you my word that whatever is in my power shall be done."

I was not sorry that my visit was drawing to a close, for it is unpleasant to feel that there is one person in the house who eagerly desires your departure. Mrs. King's sallow face and forbidding eyes had become more and more hateful to me. She was no longer actively rude—her fear of her husband prevented her—but she pushed her insane jealousy to the extent of ignoring me, never addressing me, and in every way making my stay at Greylands as uncomfortable as she could. So offensive was her manner during that last day, that I should certainly have left had it not been for that interview with my host in the evening, which would, I hoped, retrieve my broken fortunes.

It was very late when it occurred, for my relative, who had been receiving even more telegrams than usual during the day, went off to his study after dinner, and only emerged when the household had retired to bed. I heard him go round locking the doors, as his custom was of a night, and finally he joined me in the billiard-room. His stout figure was wrapped in a dressing-gown, and he wore a pair of red Turkish slippers without any heels. Settling down into an arm-chair, he brewed himself a glass of grog, in which I could not help noticing that the whisky considerably predominated over the water. "My word!" said he, "what a night!"

It was, indeed. The wind was howling and screaming round the house, and the latticed windows rattled and shook as if they were coming in. The glow of the yellow lamps and the flavour of our cigars seemed the brighter and more fragrant for the contrast.

"Now, my boy," said my host, "we have the house and the night to ourselves. Let me have an idea of how your affairs stand, and I will see what can be done to set them in order. I wish to hear every detail."

Thus encouraged, I entered into a long exposition, in which all my tradesmen and creditors, from my landlord to my valet, figured in turn. I had notes in my pocket-book, and I marshalled my facts, and gave, I flatter myself, a very business-like statement of my own unbusiness-like ways and lamentable position. I was depressed, however, to notice that my companion's eyes were vacant and his attention elsewhere. When he did occasionally throw out a remark, it was so entirely perfunctory and pointless, that I was sure he had not in the least followed my remarks. Every now and then he roused himself and put on some show of interest, asking me to repeat or to explain more fully, but it was always to sink once more into the same brown study. At last he rose and threw the end of his cigar into the grate.

"I'll tell you what, my boy," said he. "I never had a head for figures, so you will excuse me. You must jot it all down upon paper, and let me have a note of the amount. I'll understand it when I see it in black and white."

The proposal was encouraging. I promised to do so.

"And now it's time we were in bed. By Jove, there's one o'clock striking in the hall."

The tinging of the chiming clock broke through the deep roar of the gale. The wind was sweeping past with the rush of a great river.

"I must see my cat before I go to bed," said my host. "A high wind excites him. Will you come?"

"Certainly," said I.

"Then tread softly and don't speak, for everyone is asleep."

We passed quietly down the lamp-lit Persian-rugged hall, and through the door at the farther end. All was dark in the stone corridor, but a stable lantern hung on a hook, and my host took it down and lit it. There was no grating visible in the passage, so I knew that the beast was in its cage.

"Come in!" said my relative, and opened the door.

A deep growling as we entered showed that the storm had really excited the creature. In the flickering light of the lantern, we saw it, a huge black mass, coiled in the corner of its den and throwing a squat, uncouth shadow upon the whitewashed wall. Its tail switched angrily among the straw.

"Poor Tommy is not in the best of tempers," said Everard King, holding up the lantern and looking in at him.

"What a black devil he looks, doesn't he? I must give him a little supper to put him in a better humour. Would you mind holding the lantern for a moment?"

I took it from his hand and he stepped to the door.

"His larder is just outside here," said he. "You will excuse me for an instant, won't you?" He passed out, and the door shut with a sharp metallic click behind him.

That hard crisp sound made my heart stand still. A sudden wave of terror passed over me. A vague perception of some monstrous treachery turned me cold. I sprang to the door, but there was no handle upon the inner side.

"Here!" I cried. "Let me out!"

"All right! Don't make a row!" said my host from the passage. "You've got the light all right."

"Yes, but I don't care about being locked in alone like this."

"Don't you?" I heard his hearty, chuckling laugh. "You won't be alone long."

"Let me out, sir!" I repeated angrily. "I tell you I don't allow practical jokes of this sort."

"Practical is the word," said he, with another hateful chuckle. And then suddenly I heard, amidst the roar of the storm, the creak and whine of the winch-handle turning, and the rattle of the grating as it passed through the slot. Great God, he was letting loose the Brazilian cat!

In the light of the lantern I saw the bars sliding slowly before me. Already there was an opening a foot wide at the farther end. With a scream I seized the last bar with my hands and pulled with the strength of a madman. I *was* a madman with rage and horror. For a minute or more I held the thing motionless. I knew that he was straining with all his force upon the handle, and that the leverage was sure to overcome me. I gave inch by inch, my feet sliding along the stones, and all the time I begged and prayed this inhuman monster to save me from this horrible death. I conjured him by his kinship. I reminded him that I was his guest; I begged to know what harm I had ever done him. His only answers were the tugs and jerks upon the handle, each of which, in spite of all my struggles, pulled another bar through the opening. Clinging and clutching, I was dragged across the whole front of the cage, until at last, with aching wrists and lacerated fingers, I gave up the hopeless struggle. The grating clanged back as I released it, and an instant later I heard the shuffle of the Turkish slippers in the passage, and the slam of the distant door. Then everything was silent.

The creature had never moved during this time. He lay still in the corner, and his tail had ceased switching. This apparition of a man adhering to his bars and dragged screaming across him had apparently filled him with amazement. I saw his great eyes staring steadily at me. I had dropped the lantern when I seized the bars, but it still burned upon the floor, and I made a movement to grasp it, with some idea that its light might protect me. But the instant I moved, the beast gave a deep and menacing growl. I stopped and stood still, quivering with fear in every limb. The cat (if one may call so fearful a creature by so homely a name) was not more than ten feet from me. The eyes glimmered like two discs of phosphorus in the darkness. They appalled and yet fascinated me. I could not take my own eyes from them. Nature plays strange tricks with us at such moments of intensity, and those glimmering lights waxed and waned with a steady rise and fall. Sometimes they seemed to be tiny points of extreme brilliancy—little electric sparks in the black obscurity—then they would widen and widen until all that corner of the room was filled with their shifting and sinister light. And then suddenly they went out altogether.

The beast had closed its eyes. I do not know whether there may be any truth in the old idea of the dominance of the human gaze, or whether the huge cat was simply drowsy, but the fact remains that, far from showing any symptom of attacking me, it simply rested its sleek, black head upon its huge forepaws and seemed to sleep. I stood, fearing to move lest I should rouse it into malignant life once more. But at least I was able to think clearly now that the baleful eyes were off me. Here I was shut up for the night with the ferocious beast. My own instincts, to say nothing of the words of the plausible villain who laid this trap for me, warned me that the animal was as savage as its master. How could I stave it off until morning? The door was hopeless, and so were the narrow, barred windows. There was no shelter anywhere in the bare, stone-flagged room. To cry for assistance was absurd. I knew that this den was an outhouse, and that the corridor which connected it with the house was at least a hundred feet long. Besides, with that gale thundering outside, my cries were not likely to be heard. I had only my own courage and my own wits to trust to.

And then, with a fresh wave of horror, my eyes fell upon the lantern. The candle had burned low, and was already beginning to gutter. In ten minutes it would be out. I had only ten minutes then in which to do something, for I felt that if I were once left in the dark with that fearful beast I should be incapable of action. The very thought of it paralyzed me. I cast my despoiling eyes round this chamber of death, and they rested upon one spot which seemed to promise I will not say safety, but less immediate and imminent danger than the open floor.

I have said that the cage had a top as well as a front, and this top was left standing when the front was wound through the slot in the wall. It consisted of bars at a few inches' interval, with stout wire netting between, and it rested upon a strong stanchion at each end. It stood now as a great barred canopy over the crouching figure in the corner. The space between this iron shelf and the roof may have been from two to three feet. If I could only get up there, squeezed in between bars and ceiling, I should have only one vulnerable side. I should be safe from below, from behind, and from each side. Only on the open face of it could I be attacked. There, it is true, I had no protection whatever; but, at least, I should be out of the brute's path when he began to pace about his den. He would have to come out of his way to reach me. It was now or never, for if once the light were out it would be impossible. With a gulp in my throat I sprang up, seized the iron edge of the top, and swung myself panting on to it. I writhed in face downwards, and found myself looking straight into the terrible eyes and yawning jaws of the cat. Its fetid breath came up into my face like the steam from some foul pot.

It appeared, however, to be rather curious than angry. With a sleek ripple of its long, black back it rose, stretched itself, and then rearing itself on its hind legs, with one fore-paw against the wall, it raised the other, and drew its claws across the wire meshes beneath me. One sharp, white hook tore through my trousers—for I may mention that I was still in evening dress—and dug a furrow in my knee. It was not meant as an attack, but rather as an experiment, for upon my giving a sharp cry of pain he dropped down again, and springing lightly into the room, he began walking swiftly round it, looking up every now and again in my direction. For my part I shuffled backwards until I lay with my back against the wall, screwing myself into the smallest space possible. The farther I got, the more difficult it was for him to attack me.

He seemed more excited now that he had begun to move about, and he ran swiftly and noiselessly round and round the den, passing continually underneath the iron couch upon which I lay. It was wonderful to see so great a bulk passing like a shadow, with hardly the softest thudding of velvety pads. The candle was burning low—so low that I could hardly see the creature. And then, with a last flare and splutter it went out altogether. I was alone with the cat in the dark.

It helps one to face a danger when one knows that one has done all that possibly can be done. There is nothing for it then but to quietly await the result. In this case, there was no chance of safety anywhere except the precise spot where I was. I stretched myself out, therefore, and lay silently, almost breathlessly, hoping that the beast might forget my presence if I did nothing to remind him. I reckoned that it must already be two o'clock. At four it would be full dawn. I had not more than two hours to wait for daylight.

Outside, the storm was still raging, and the rain lashed continually against the little windows. Inside, the poisonous and fetid air was overpowering. I could neither hear nor see the cat. I tried to think about other things—but only one had power enough to draw my mind from my terrible position. That was the contemplation of my cousin's villainy, his unparalleled hypocrisy, his malignant hatred of me. Beneath that cheerful face there lurked the spirit of a medieval assassin. And as I thought of it I saw more clearly how cunningly the thing had been arranged. He had apparently gone to bed with the others. No doubt he had his witnesses to prove it. Then, unknown to them, he had slipped down, had lured me into this den and abandoned me. His story would be so simple. He had left me to finish my cigar in the billiard-room. I had gone down on my own account to have a last look at the cat. I had entered the room without observing that the cage was opened, and I had been caught. How could such a crime be brought home to him? Suspicion, perhaps—but proof, never!

How slowly those dreadful two hours went by! Once I heard a low, rasping sound, which I took to be the creature licking its own fur. Several times those greenish eyes gleamed at me through the darkness, but never in a fixed stare, and my hopes grew stronger that my presence had been forgotten or ignored. At last the least faint glimmer of light came through the windows—I first dimly saw them as two grey squares upon the black wall, then grey turned to white, and I could see my terrible companion once more. And he, alas, could see me!

It was evident to me at once that he was in a much more dangerous and aggressive mood than when I had seen him last. The cold of the morning had irritated him, and he was hungry as well. With a continual growl he paced swiftly up and down the side of the room which was farthest from my refuge, his whiskers bristling angrily, and his tail switching and lashing. As he turned at the corners his savage eyes always looked upwards at me with a dreadful menace. I knew then that he meant to kill me. Yet I found myself even at that moment admiring the sinuous grace of the devilish thing, its long, undulating, rippling movements, the gloss of its beautiful flanks, the vivid, palpitating scarlet of the glistening tongue which hung from the jet-black muzzle. And all the time that deep, threatening growl was rising and rising in an unbroken crescendo. I knew that the crisis was at hand.

It was a miserable hour to meet such a death—so cold, so comfortless, shivering in my light dress clothes upon this gridiron of torment upon which I was stretched. I tried to brace myself to it, to raise my soul above it, and at the same time, with the lucidity which comes to a perfectly desperate man, I cast round for some possible means of escape. One thing was clear to me. If that front of the cage was only back in its position once more, I could find a sure refuge behind it. Could I possibly pull it back? I hardly dared to move for fear of bringing the creature upon me. Slowly, very slowly, I put my hand forward until it grasped the edge of the front, the final bar which protruded through the wall. To my surprise it came quite easily to my jerk. Of course the difficulty of drawing it out arose from the fact that I was clinging to it. I pulled again, and three inches of it came through. It ran apparently on wheels. I pulled again . . . and then the cat sprang!

It was so quick, so sudden, that I never saw it happen. I simply heard the savage snarl, and in an instant afterwards the blazing yellow eyes, the flattened black head with its red tongue and flashing teeth, were within reach of me. The impact of the creature shook the bars upon which I lay, until I thought (as far as I could think of anything at such a moment) that they were coming down. The cat swayed there for an instant, the head and front paws quite close to me, the hind paws clawing to find a grip upon the edge of the grating. I heard the claws rasping as they clung to the wire netting, and the breath of the beast made me sick. But its bound had been miscalculated. It could not retain its position. Slowly, grinning with rage and scratching madly at the bars, it swung backwards and dropped heavily upon the floor. With a growl it instantly faced round to me and crouched for another spring.

I knew that the next few moments would decide my fate. The creature had learned by experience. It would not miscalculate again. I must act promptly, fearlessly, if I were to have a chance for life. In an instant I had formed my plan. Pulling off my dress-coat, I threw it down over the head of the beast. At the same moment I dropped over the edge, seized the end of the front grating, and pulled it frantically out of the wall.

It came more easily than I could have expected. I rushed across the room, bearing it with me; but, as I rushed, the accident of my position put me upon the outer side. Had it been the other way, I might have come off scathless. As it was, there was a moment's pause as I stopped it and tried to pass in through the opening which I had left. That moment was enough to give time to the creature to toss off the coat with which I had blinded him and to spring upon me. I hurled myself through the gap and pulled the rails to behind me, but he seized my leg before I could entirely withdraw it. One stroke of that huge paw tore off my calf as a shaving of wood curls off before a plane. The next moment, bleeding and fainting, I was lying among the foul straw with a line of friendly bars between me and the creature which ramped so frantically against them.

Too wounded to move, and too faint to be conscious of fear, I could only lie, more dead than alive, and watch it. It pressed its broad, black chest against the bars and angled for me with its crooked paws as I have seen a kitten do before a mouse-trap. It ripped my clothes, but, stretch as it would, it could not quite reach me. I have heard of the curious numbing effect produced by wounds from the great carnivora, and now I was destined to experience it, for I had lost all sense of personality, and was as interested in the cat's failure or success as if it were some game which I was watching. And then gradually my mind drifted away into strange, vague dreams, always with that black face and red tongue coming back into them, and so I lost myself in the nirvana of delirium, the blessed relief of those who are too sorely tried.

Tracing the course of events afterwards, I conclude that I must have been insensible for about two hours. What roused me to consciousness once more was that sharp metallic click which had been the precursor of my terrible experience. It was the shooting back of the spring lock. Then, before my senses were clear enough to entirely apprehend what they saw, I was aware of the round, benevolent face of my cousin peering in through the opened door. What he saw evidently amazed him. There was the cat crouching on the floor. I was stretched upon my back in my shirt sleeves within the cage, my trousers torn to ribbons and a great pool of blood all round me. I can see his amazed face now, with the morning sunlight upon it. He peered at me, and peered again. Then he closed the door behind him, and advanced to the cage to see if I were really dead.

I cannot undertake to say what happened. I was not in a fit state to witness or to chronicle such events. I can only say that I was suddenly conscious that his face was away from me—that he was looking towards the animal.

"Good old Tommy!" he cried. "Good old Tommy!"

Then he came near the bars, with his back still towards me.

"Down, you stupid beast!" he roared. "Down, sir! Don't you know your master?"

Suddenly even in my bemuddled brain a remembrance came of those words of his when he had said that the taste of blood would turn the cat into a fiend. My blood had done it, but he was to pay the price.

"Get away!" he screamed. "Get away, you devil! Baldwin! Baldwin! Oh, my God!"

And then I heard him fall, and rise, and fall again, with a sound like the ripping of sacking. His screams grew fainter until they were lost in the worrying snarl. And then, after I thought that he was dead, I saw, as in a nightmare, a blinded, tattered, blood-soaked figure running wildly round the room—and that was the last glimpse which I had of him before I fainted once again.

I was many months in my recovery—in fact, I cannot say that I have ever recovered, for to the end of my days I shall carry a stick as a sign of my night with the Brazilian cat. Baldwin, the groom, and the other servants could not tell what had occurred when, drawn by the death cries of their master, they found me behind the bars, and his remains—or what they afterwards discovered to be his remains—in the clutch of the creature which he had reared. They stalled him off with hot irons, and afterwards shot him through the loophole of the door before they could finally extricate me. I was carried to my bedroom, and there, under the roof of my would-be murderer, I remained between life and death for several weeks. They had sent for a surgeon from Clipton and a nurse from London, and in a month I was able to be carried to the station, and so conveyed back once more to Grosvenor Mansions.

I have one remembrance of that illness, which might have been part of the ever-changing panorama conjured up by a delirious brain were it not so definitely fixed in my memory. One night, when the nurse was absent, the door of my chamber opened, and a tall woman in blackest mourning slipped into the room. She came across to me, and as she bent her sallow face I saw by the faint gleam of the night-light that it was the Brazilian woman whom my cousin had married. She stared intently into my face, and her expression was more kindly than I had ever seen it.

"Are you conscious?" she asked.

I feebly nodded—for I was still very weak.

"Well, then, I only wished to say to you that you have yourself to blame. Did I not do all I could for you? From the beginning I tried to drive you from the house. By every means, short of betraying my husband, I tried to save you from him. I knew that he had a reason for bringing you here. I knew that he would never let you get away again. No one knew him as I knew him, who had suffered from him so often. I did not dare to tell you all this. He would have killed me. But I did my best for you. As things have turned out, you have been the best friend that I have ever had. You have set me free, and I fancied that nothing but death would do that. I am sorry if you are hurt, but I cannot reproach myself. I told you that you were a fool— and a fool you have been." She crept out of the room, the bitter, singular woman, and I was never destined to see her again. With what remained from her husband's property she went back to her native land, and I have heard that she afterwards took the veil at Pernambuco.

It was not until I had been back in London for some time that the doctors pronounced me to be well enough to do business. It was not a very welcome permission to me, for I feared that it would be the signal for an inrush of creditors; but it was Summers, my lawyer, who first took advantage of it.

"I am very glad to see that your lordship is so much better," said he. "I have been waiting a long time to offer my congratulations."

"What do you mean, Summers? This is no time for joking."

"I mean what I say," he answered. "You have been Lord Southerton for the last six weeks, but we feared that it would retard your recovery if you were to learn it."

Lord Southerton! One of the richest peers in England! I could not believe my ears. And then suddenly I thought of the time which had elapsed, and how it coincided with my injuries.

"Then Lord Southerton must have died about the same time that I was hurt?"

"His death occurred upon that very day." Summers looked hard at me as I spoke, and I am convinced—for he was a very shrewd fellow—that he had guessed the true state of the case. He paused for a moment as if awaiting a confidence from me, but I could not see what was to be gained by exposing such a family scandal.

"Yes, a very curious coincidence," he continued, with the same knowing look. "Of course, you are unaware that your cousin Everard King was the next heir to the estates. Now, if it had been you instead of him who had been torn to pieces by this tiger, or whatever it was, then of course he would have been Lord Southerton at the present moment."

"No doubt," said I.

"And he took such an interest in it," said Summers. "I happen to know that the late Lord Southerton's valet was in his pay, and that he used to have telegrams from him every few hours to tell him how he was getting on. That would be about the time when you were down there. Was it not strange that he should wish to be so well informed, since he knew that he was not the direct heir?"

"Very strange," said I. "And now, Summers, if you will bring me my bills and a new cheque-book, we will begin to get things into order."

/ B.24 /

I told my story when I was taken, and no one would
listen to me. Then I told it again at the trial—the whole
thing absolutely as it happened, without so much as a word
added. I set it all out truly, so help me God, all that Lady
Mannering said and did, and then all that I had said and
done, just as it occurred. And what did I get for it? "The
prisoner put forward a rambling and inconsequential statement, incredible in its details, and unsupported by any shred
of corroborating evidence." That was what one of the London papers said, and others let it pass as if I had made no
defence at all. And yet, with my own eyes I saw Lord
Mannering murdered, and I am as guiltless of it as any
man on the jury that tried me.

Now, sir, you are there to receive the petitions of pris-
oners. It all lies with you. All I ask is that you read it—just
read it—and then that you make an inquiry or two about
the private character of this "lady" Mannering, if she still
keeps the name that she had three years ago, when to my
sorrow and ruin I came to meet her. You could use a private inquiry agent or a good lawyer, and you would soon
learn enough to show you that my story is the true one.

Think of the glory it would be to you to have all the papers saying that there would have been a shocking miscarriage of justice if it had not been for your perseverance and intelligence! That must be your reward, since I am a poor man and can offer you nothing. But if you don't do it, may you never lie easy in your bed again! May no night pass that you are not haunted by the thought of the man who rots in gaol because you have not done the duty which you are paid to do! But you will do it, sir, I know. Just make one or two inquiries, and you will soon find which way the wind blows. Remember, also, that the only person who profited by the crime was herself, since it changed her from an unhappy wife to a rich young widow. There's the end of the string in your hand, and you only have to follow it up and see where it leads to.

Mind you, sir, I make no complaint as far as the burglary goes. I don't whine about what I have deserved, and so far I have had no more than I have deserved. Burglary it was, right enough, and my three years have gone to pay for it. It was shown at the trial that I had had a hand in the Merton Cross business, and did a year for that, so my story had the less attention on that account. A man with a previous conviction never gets a really fair trial. I own to the burglary, but when it comes to the murder which brought me a lifer—any judge but Sir James might have given me the gallows—then I tell you that I had nothing to do with it, and that I am an innocent man. And now I'll take that night, the 13th of September, 1894, and I'll give you just exactly what occurred, and may God's hand strike me down if I go one inch over the truth.

I had been at Bristol in the summer looking for work, and then I had a notion that I might get something at Portsmouth, for I was trained as a skilled mechanic, so I came tramping my way across the south of England, and doing odd jobs as I went. I was trying all I knew to keep off the cross, for I had done a year in Exeter Gaol, and I had had enough of visiting Queen Victoria. But it's cruel hard to get work when once the black mark is against your name, and it was all I could do to keep soul and body together. At last, after ten days of wood-cutting and stone-breaking on starvation pay, I found myself near Salisbury with a couple of shillings in my pocket, and my boots and my patience clean wore out. There's an ale-house called "The Willing Mind," which stands on the road between Blandford and Salisbury, and it was there that night I engaged a bed. I was sitting alone in the tap room just about closing time, when the innkeeper—Allen his name was—came beside me and began yarning about the neighbours. He was a man that liked to talk and to have some one to listen to him talk, so I sat there smoking and drinking a mug of ale which he had stood me; and I took no great interest in what he said until he began to talk (as the devil would have it) about the riches of Mannering Hall.

"Meaning the large house on the right before I came to the village?" said I. "The one that stands in its own park?"

"Exactly," said he—and I am giving all our talk so that you may know that I am telling you the truth and hiding nothing. "The long white house with the pillars," said he. "At the side of the Blandford Road."

Now I had looked at it as I passed, and it had crossed my mind, as such thoughts will, that it was a very easy house to get into with that great row of ground windows and glass doors. I had put the thought away from me, and now here was this landlord bringing it back with his talk about the riches within. I said nothing, but I listened, and as luck would have it, he would always come back to this one subject.

"He was a miser young, so you can think what he is now in his age," said he. "Well, he's had some good out of his money."

"What good can he have had if he does not spend it?" said I.

"Well, it bought him the prettiest wife in England, and that was some good that he got out of it. She thought she would have the spending of it, but she knows the difference now."

"Who was she then?" I asked, just for the sake of something to say.

"She was nobody at all until the old Lord made her his Lady," said he. "She came from up London way, and some said that she had been on the stage there, but nobody knew. The old Lord was away for a year, and when he came home he brought a young wife back with him, and there she has been ever since. Stephens, the butler, did tell me once that she was the light of the house when first she came, but what with her husband's mean and aggravatin' way, and what with her loneliness—for he hates to see a visitor within his doors; and what with his bitter words—for he has a tongue like a hornet's sting, her life all went out of her, and she became a white, silent creature, moping about the country lanes. Some say that she loved another man, and that it was just the riches of the old Lord which tempted her to be false to her lover, and that now she is eating her heart out because she has lost the one without being any nearer to the other, for she might be the poorest woman in the parish for all the money that she has the handling of."

Well, sir, you can imagine that it did not interest me very much to hear about the quarrels between a Lord and a Lady. What did it matter to me if she hated the sound of his voice, or if he put every indignity upon her in the hope of breaking her spirit, and spoke to her as he would never have dared to speak to one of his servants? The landlord told me of these things, and of many more like them, but they passed out of my mind, for they were no concern of mine. But what I did want to hear was the form in which Lord Mannering kept his riches. Title-deeds and stock certificates are but paper, and more danger than profit to the man who takes them. But metal and stones are worth a risk. And then, as if he were answering my very thoughts, the landlord told me of Lord Mannering's great collection of gold medals, that it was the most valuable in the world, and that it was reckoned that if they were put into a sack the strongest man in the parish would not be able to raise them. Then his wife called him, and he and I went to our beds.

I am not arguing to make out a case for myself, but I beg you, sir, to bear all the facts in your mind, and to ask yourself whether a man could be more sorely tempted than I was. I make bold to say that there are few who could have held out against it. There I lay on my bed that night, a desperate man without hope or work, and with my last shilling in my pocket. I had tried to be honest, and honest folk had turned their backs upon me. They taunted me for theft; and yet they pushed me towards it. I was caught in the stream and could not get out. And then it was such a chance: the great house all lined with windows, the golden medals which could so easily be melted down. It was like putting a loaf before a starving man and expecting him not to eat it. I fought against it for a time, but it was no use. At last I sat up on the side of my bed, and I swore that that night I should either be a rich man and able to give up crime for ever, or that the irons should be on my wrists once more. Then I slipped on my clothes, and, having put a shilling on the table—for the landlord had treated me well, and I did not wish to cheat him—I passed out through the window into the garden of the inn.

There was a high wall round this garden, and I had a job to get over it, but once on the other side it was all plain sailing. I did not meet a soul upon the road, and the iron gate of the avenue was open. No one was moving at the lodge. The moon was shining, and I could see the great house glimmering white through an archway of trees. I walked up it for a quarter of a mile or so, until I was at the edge of the drive, where it ended in a broad, gravelled space before the main door. There I stood in the shadow and looked at the long building, with a full moon shining in every window and silvering the high stone front. I crouched there for some time, and I wondered where I should find the easiest entrance. The corner window of the side seemed to be the one which was least overlooked, and a screen of ivy hung heavily over it. My best chance was evidently there. I worked my way under the trees to the back of the house, and then crept along in the black shadow of the building. A dog barked and rattled his chain, but I stood waiting until he was quiet, and then I stole on once more until I came to the window which I had chosen.

It is astonishing how careless they are in the country, in places far removed from large towns, where the thought of burglars never enters their heads. I call it setting temptation in a poor man's way when he puts his hand, meaning no harm, upon a door, and finds it swing open before him. In this case it was not so bad as that, but the window was merely fastened with the ordinary catch, which I opened with a push from the blade of my knife. I pulled up the window as quickly as possible, and then I thrust the knife through the slit in the shutter and prized it open. They were folding shutters, and I shoved them before me and walked into the room.

"Good evening, sir! You are very welcome!" said a voice.

I've had some starts in my life, but never one to come up to that one. There, in the opening of the shutters, within reach of my arm, was standing a woman with a small coil of wax taper burning in her hand. She was tall and straight and slender, with a beautiful white face that might have been cut out of clear marble, but her hair and eyes were as black as night. She was dressed in some sort of white dressing-gown which flowed down to her feet, and what with this robe and what with her face, it seemed as if a spirit from above was standing in front of me. My knees knocked together, and I held on to the shutter with one hand to give me support. I should have turned and run away if I had had the strength, but I could only just stand and stare at her. She soon brought me back to myself once more.

"Don't be frightened!" said she, and they were strange words for the mistress of a house to have to use to a burglar. "I saw you out of my bedroom window when you were hiding under those trees, so I slipped downstairs, and then I heard you at the window. I should have opened it for you if you had waited, but you managed it yourself just as I came up."

I still held in my hand the long clasp-knife with which I had opened the shutter. I was unshaven and grimed from a week on the roads. Altogether, there are few people who would have cared to face me alone at one in the morning; but this woman, if I had been her lover meeting her by appointment, could not have looked upon me with a more welcoming eye. She laid her hand upon my sleeve and drew me into the room.

"What's the meaning of this, ma'am? Don't get trying any little games upon me," said I, in my roughest way— and I can put it on rough when I like. "It'll be the worse for you if you play me any trick," I added, showing her my knife.

"I will play you no trick," said she. "On the contrary, I am your friend, and I wish to help you."

"Excuse me, ma'am, but I find it hard to believe that," said I. "Why should you wish to help me?"

"I have my own reasons," said she; and then suddenly, with those black eyes blazing out of her white face: "It's because I hate him, hate him, hate him! Now you understand."

I remembered what the landlord had told me, and I did understand. I looked at her Ladyship's face, and I knew that I could trust her. She wanted to revenge herself upon her husband. She wanted to hit him where it would hurt him most—upon the pocket. She hated him so that she would even lower her pride to take such a man as me into her confidence if she could gain her end by doing so. I've hated some folk in my time, but I don't think I ever understood what hate was until I saw that woman's face in the light of the taper.

"You'll trust me now?" said she, with another coaxing touch upon my sleeve.

"Yes, your Ladyship."

"You know me, then."

"I can guess who you are."

"I daresay my wrongs are the talk of the county. But what does he care for that? He only cares for one thing in the whole world, and that you can take from him this night. Have you a bag?"

"No, your Ladyship."

"Shut the shutter behind you. Then no one can see the light. You are quite safe. The servants all sleep in the other wing. I can show you where all the most valuable things are. You cannot carry them all. So we must pick the best."

The room in which I found myself was long and low, with many rugs and skins scattered about on a polished wood floor. Small cases stood here and there, and the walls were decorated with spears and swords and paddles, and other things which find their way into museums. There were some queer clothes, too, which had been brought from savage countries, and the lady took down a large leather sack-bag from among them.

"This sleeping-sack will do," said she. "Now come with me and I will show you where the medals are."

It was like a dream to me to think that this tall, white woman was the lady of the house, and that she was lending me a hand to rob her own home. I could have burst out laughing at the thought of it, and yet there was something in that pale face of hers which stopped my laughter and turned me cold and serious. She swept on in front of me like a spirit, with the green taper in her hand, and I walked behind with my sack until we came to a door at the end of this museum. It was locked, but the key was in it, and she led me through.

The room beyond was a small one, hung all round with curtains which had pictures on them. It was the hunting of a deer that was painted on it, as I remember, and in the flicker of that light you'd have sworn that the dogs and the horses were streaming round the walls. The only other thing in the room was a row of cases made of walnut, with brass ornaments. They had glass tops, and beneath this glass I saw the long lines of those gold medals, some of them as big as a plate and half an inch thick, all resting upon red velvet and glowing and gleaming in the darkness. My fingers were just itching to be at them, and I slipped my knife under the lock of one of the cases to wrench it open.

"Wait a moment," said she, laying her hand upon my arm. "You might do better than this."

"I am very well satisfied, ma'am," said I, "and much obliged to your Ladyship for kind assistance."

"You can do better," she repeated. "Would not golden sovereigns be worth more to you than these things?"

"Why, yes," said I. "That's best of all."

"Well," said she. "He sleeps just above our head. It is but one short staircase. There is a tin box with money enough to fill this bag under his bed."

"How can I get it without waking him?"

"What matter if he does wake?" She looked very hard at me as she spoke. "You could keep him from calling out."

"No, no, ma'am, I'll have none of that."

"Just as you like," said she. "I thought that you were a stout-hearted sort of man by your appearance, but I see that I made a mistake. If you are afraid to run the risk of one old man, then of course you cannot have the gold which is under his bed. You are the best judge of your own business, but I should think that you would do better at some other trade."

"I'll not have murder on my conscience."

"You could overpower him without harming him. I never said anything of murder. The money lies under the bed. But if you are faint-hearted, it is better that you should not attempt it."

She worked upon me so, partly with her scorn and partly with this money that she held before my eyes, that I believe I should have yielded and taken my chances upstairs, had it not been that I saw her eyes following the struggle within me in such a crafty, malignant fashion, that it was evident she was bent upon making me the tool of her revenge, and that she would leave me no choice but to do the old man an injury or to be captured by him. She felt suddenly that she was giving herself away, and she changed her face to a kindly, friendly smile, but it was too late, for I had had my warning.

"I will not go upstairs," said I. "I have all I want here."

She looked her contempt at me, and there never was a face which could look it plainer.

"Very good. You can take these medals. I should be glad if you would begin at this end. I suppose they will all be the same value when melted down, but these are the ones which are the rarest, and, therefore, the most precious to him. It is not necessary to break the locks. If you press that brass knob you will find that there is a secret spring. So! Take that small one first—it is the very apple of his eye."

She had opened one of the cases, and the beautiful things all lay exposed before me. I had my hand upon the one which she had pointed out, when suddenly a change came over her face, and she held up one finger as a warning. "Hist!" she whispered. "What is that?"

Far away in the silence of the house we heard a low, dragging, shuffling sound, and the distant tread of feet, She closed and fastened the case in an instant.

"It's my husband!" she whispered. "All right. Don't be alarmed. I'll arrange it. Here! Quick, behind the tapestry!"

She pushed me behind the painted curtains upon the wall, my empty leather bag still in my hand. Then she took her taper and walked quickly into the room from which we had come. From where I stood I could see her through the open door.

"Is that you, Robert?" she cried.

The light of a candle shone through the door of the museum, and the shuffling steps came nearer and nearer. Then I saw a face in the doorway, a great, heavy face, all lines and creases, with a huge curving nose, and a pair of gold glasses fixed across it. He had to throw his head back to see through the glasses, and that great nose thrust out in front of him like the beak of some sort of fowl. He was a big man, very tall and burly, so that in his loose dressing-gown his figure seemed to fill up the whole doorway. He had a pile of grey, curling hair all round his head, but his face was clean shaven. His mouth was thin and small and prim, hidden way under his long, masterful nose. He stood there, holding the candle in front of him, and looking at his wife with a queer, malicious gleam in his eyes. It only needed that one look to tell me that he was as fond of her as she was of him.

"How's this?" he asked. "Some new tantrum? What do you mean by wandering about the house? Why don't you go to bed?"

"I could not sleep," she answered. She spoke languidly and wearily. If she was an actress once, she had not forgotten her calling.

"Might I suggest," said he, in the same mocking kind of voice, "that a good conscience is an excellent aid to sleep?"

"That cannot be true," she answered, "for you sleep very well."

"I have only one thing in my life to be ashamed of," said he, and his hair bristled up with anger until he looked like an old cockatoo. "You know best what that is. It is a mistake which has brought its own punishment with it."

"To me as well as to you. Remember that!"

"You have very little to whine about. It was I who stooped and you who rose."

"Rose!"

"Yes, rose. I suppose you do not deny that it is promotion to exchange the music-hall for Mannering Hall. Fool that I was ever to take you out of your true sphere!"

"If you think so, why do you not separate?"

"Because private misery is better than public humiliation; because it is easier to suffer for a mistake than to own to it. Because also I like to keep you in my sight, and to know that you cannot go back to him."

"You villain! You cowardly villain!"

"Yes, yes, my lady. I know your secret ambition, but it shall never be while I live, and if it happens after my death I will at least take care that you go to him as a beggar. You and dear Edward will never have the satisfaction of squandering my savings, and you may make up your mind to that, my lady. Why are those shutters and the window open?"

"I found the night very close."

"It is not safe. How do you know that some tramp may not be outside? Are you aware that my collection of medals is worth more than any similar collection in this world? You have left the door open also. What is there to prevent any one from rifling the cases?"

"I was here."

"I know you were. I heard you moving about in the medal room, and that was why I came down. What were you doing?"

"Looking at the medals. What else should I be doing?"

"This curiosity is something new." He looked suspiciously at her and moved on towards the inner room, she walking beside him.

It was at this moment that I saw something which startled me. I had laid my clasp-knife open upon the top of one of the cases, and there it lay in full view. She saw it before he did, and with a woman's cunning she held her taper out so that the light of it came between Lord Mannering's eyes and the knife. Then she took it in her left hand and held it against her gown out of his sight. He looked about from case to case—I could have put my hand at one time upon his long nose—but there was nothing to show that the medals had been tampered with, and so, still snarling and grumbling, he shuffled off into the other room once more.

And now I have to speak of what I heard rather than of what I saw, but I swear to you, as I shall stand some day before my Maker, that what I say is the truth.

When they passed into the outer room I saw him lay his candle upon the corner of one of the tables, and he sat himself down, but in such a position that he was just out of my sight. She moved behind him, as I could tell from the fact that the light of her taper threw his long, lumpy shadow upon the floor in front of him. Then he began talking about this man whom he called Edward, and every word that he said was like a blistering drop of vitriol. He spoke low, so that I could not hear it all, but from what I heard I should guess that she would as soon have been lashed with a whip. At first she said some hot words in reply, but then she was silent, and he went on and on in that cold, mocking voice of his, nagging and insulting and tormenting, until I wondered that she could bear to stand there in silence and listen to it. Then suddenly I heard him say in a sharp voice, "Come from behind me! Leave go of my collar! What! would you dare to strike me?" There was a sound like a blow, just a soft sort of thud, and then I heard him cry out, "My God, it's blood!" He shuffled with his feet as if he was getting up, and then I heard another blow, and he cried out, "Oh, you she-devil!" and was quiet, except for a dripping and splashing upon the floor.

I ran out from behind my curtain at that, and rushed into the other room, shaking all over with the horror of it. The old man had slipped down in the chair, and his dressing-gown had rucked up until he looked as if he had a monstrous hump to his back. His head, with the gold glasses still fixed on his nose, was lolling over upon one side, and his little mouth was open just like a dead fish. I could not see where the blood was coming from, but I could still hear it drumming upon the floor. She stood behind him with the candle shining full upon her face. Her lips were pressed together and her eyes shining, and a touch of colour had come into each of her cheeks. It just wanted that to make her the most beautiful woman I had ever seen in my life.

"You've done it now!" said I.

"Yes," said she, in her quiet way, "I've done it now."

"What are you going to do?" I asked. "They'll have you for murder as sure as fate."

"Never fear about me. I have nothing to live for, and it does not matter. Give me a hand to set him straight in the chair. It is horrible to see him like this!"

I did so, though it turned me cold all over to touch him. Some of his blood came on my hand and sickened me.

"Now," said she, "you may as well have the medals as anyone else. Take them and go."

"I don't want them. I only want to get away. I was never mixed up with a business like this before."

"Nonsense!" said she. "You came for the medals, and here they are at your mercy. Why should you not have them? There is no one to prevent you."

I held the bag, still in my hand. She opened the case, and between us we threw a hundred or so of the medals into it. They were all from the one case, but I could not bring myself to wait for any more. Then I made for the window, for the very air of this house seemed to poison me after what I had seen and heard. As I looked back, I saw her standing there, tall and graceful, with the light in her hand, just as I had seen her first. She waved good-bye, and I waved back at her and sprang out into the gravel drive.

I thank God that I can lay my hand upon my heart and say that I have never done a murder, but perhaps it would be different if I had been able to read that woman's mind and thoughts. There might have been two bodies in the room instead of one if I could have seen behind that last smile of hers. But I thought of nothing but of getting safely away, and it never entered my head how she might be fixing the rope round my neck. I had not taken five steps out from the window skirting down the shadow of the house in the way that I had come, when I heard a scream that might have raised the parish, and then another and another.

"Murder!" she cried. "Murder! Murder! Help!" and her voice rang out in the quiet of the night-time and sounded over the whole countryside. It went through my head, that dreadful cry. In an instant lights began to move and windows to fly up, not only in the house behind me, but at the

lodge and in the stables in front. Like a frightened rabbit I
bolted down the drive, but I heard the clang of the gate
being shut before I could reach it. Then I hid my bag of
medals under some dry fagots, and I tried to get away across
the park, but some one saw me in the moonlight, and presently I had half a dozen of them with dogs upon my heels.
I crouched down among the brambles, but those dogs were
too many for me, and I was glad enough when the men
came up and prevented me from being torn into pieces.
They seized me, and dragged me back to the room from
which I had come.

"Is this the man, your Ladyship?" asked the oldest of
them—the same whom I found out afterwards to be the
butler.

She had been bending over the body, with her handkerchief to her eyes, and now she turned upon me with the
face of a fury. Oh, what an actress that woman was!

"Yes, yes, it is the very man," she cried. "Oh, you villain, you cruel villain, to treat an old man so!"

There was a man there who seemed to be a village
constable. He laid his hand upon my shoulder.

"What do you say to that?" said he.

"It was she who did it," I cried, pointing at the woman,
whose eyes never flinched before mine.

"Come! Come! Try another!" said the constable, and
one of the men-servants struck at me with his fist.

"I tell you that I saw her do it. She stabbed him twice
with a knife. She first helped me to rob him, and then she
murdered him."

The footman tried to strike me again, but she held up her hand.

"Do not hurt him," said she. "I think that his punishment may safely be left to the law."

"I'll see to that, your Ladyship," said the constable. "Your Ladyship actually saw the crime committed, did you not?"

"Yes, yes, I saw it with my own eyes. It was horrible. We heard the noise and we came down. My poor husband was in front. The man had one of the cases open, and was filling a black leather bag, which he held in his hand. He rushed past us, and my husband seized him. There was a struggle, and he stabbed him twice. There you can see the blood upon his hands. If I am not mistaken, his knife is still in Lord Mannering's body."

"Look at the blood upon her hands!" I cried.

"She has been holding up his Lordship's head, you lying rascal," said the butler.

"And here's the very sack her Ladyship spoke of," said the constable, as a groom came in with the one which I had dropped in my flight. "And here are the medals inside it. That's good enough for me. We will keep him safe here tonight, and tomorrow the inspector and I can take him into Salisbury."

"Poor creature," said the woman. "For my own part, I forgive him any injury which he has done me. Who knows what temptation may have driven him to crime? His conscience and the law will give him punishment enough without any reproach of mine rendering it more bitter."

I could not answer—I tell you, sir, I could not answer, so taken aback was I by the assurance of the woman. And so, seeming by my silence to agree to all that she had said, I was dragged away by the butler and the constable into the cellar, in which they locked me for the night.

There, sir, I have told you the whole story of the events which led up to the murder of Lord Mannering by his wife upon the night of September the 14th, in the year 1894. Perhaps you will put my statement on one side as the constable did at Mannering Towers, or the judge afterwards at the county assizes. Or perhaps you will see that there is the ring of truth in what I say, and you will follow it up, and so make your name forever as a man who does not grudge personal trouble where justice is to be done. I have only you to look to, sir, and if you will clear my name of this false accusation, then I will worship you as one man never yet worshipped another. But if you fail me, then I give you my solemn promise that I will rope myself up, this day month, to the bar of my window, and from that time on I will come to plague you in your dreams if ever yet one man was able to come back and to haunt another. What I ask you to do is very simple. Make inquiries about this woman, watch her, learn her past history, find out what use she is making of the money which has come to her, and whether there is not a man Edward as I have stated. If from all this you learn anything which shows you her real character, or which seems to you to corroborate the story which I have told you, then I am sure that I can rely upon your goodness of heart to come to the rescue of an innocent man.